Village of Stone

XIAOLU GUO

Village of Stone

Translated from Chinese by
Cindy Carter

Chatto & Windus
LONDON

Published by Chatto & Windus 2004

2 4 6 8 10 9 7 5 3 1

Copyright © Xiaolu Guo 2004

Xiaolu Guo has asserted her right under the Copyright, Designs
and Patents Act, 1988 to be identified as the author of this work

First published in Great Britain in 2004 by
Chatto & Windus
Random House, 20 Vauxhall Bridge Road,
London SW1V 2SA

Random House Australia (Pty) Limited
20 Alfred Street, Milsons Point, Sydney,
New South Wales 2061, Australia

Random House New Zealand Limited
18 Poland Road, Glenfield,
Auckland 10, New Zealand

Random House (Pty) Limited
Endulini, 5a Jubilee Road, Parktown 2193, South Africa

The Random House Group Limited Reg. No. 954009
www.randomhouse.co.uk

A CIP catalogue record for this book
is available from the British Library

ISBN 0 7011 7604 0

Papers used by Random House are natural,
recyclable products made from wood grown in sustainable forests;
the manufacturing processes conform to the environmental
regulations of the country of origin

Typeset by Palimpsest Book Production Ltd,
Polmont, Stirlingshire
Printed and bound in Great Britain by
Mackays of Chatham plc, Chatham, Kent

To my home town, Shi Tang,
where everything began

I see myself on a boat, steering out to sea, to the seas of the Village of Stone. As the waves grow clearer in my memory, I find myself moving farther away from this enormous city, these enormous buildings and enormous crowds . . . Scattering torpedoes as I go, I storm the secret fortresses of my soul, conquering them one by one, as explosions reverberate through my eardrums and shattered whitecaps drench my clothes. Soon all this subsides, drifting down to the deepest seafloor, torpedoes still exploding into schools of cruising fish. The sea turns red and I feel pain – all those fish, I never wanted them to die . . . I stand on the deck weeping, watching my tears fall into the sea, the sea of the Village of Stone, this place where I bury my fish, my memories, my childhood, and all the secrets of my past incarnation . . .

Xiaolu Guo
Autumn, 2000

I

It all started with a parcel of dried eel. A parcel of dried, salted eel posted by some nameless sender from some unknown address in the Village of Stone.

It is a large marine eel, approximately eighty-five centimetres in length, with the dorsal, rear and tail fins still attached. The tail fin is extraordinarily long. I imagine that the eel must have been prepared in the traditional manner of the Village of Stone, which means that it would have been dried in the sun after being salted with two kilograms of coarse sea salt for each five kilograms of eel. You can still see the scar where the blade of the knife sliced into the eel's silvery-white belly, before being pulled out again to shear the eel slowly from head to tail, shaping it into a pair of long strips connected at the centre.

Such an enormous eel, I decide, must have been caught during the seventh moon of the lunar calendar, when eels are said to be at their plumpest and most delicious. The eel would first have had its entrails pulled out and then been hung from a north-facing window to dry for the duration of the winter fishing season. When it had hardened to the consistency of a knife blade, some hand – whose hand I know not – must have taken it down from the rafters, parcelled it up and mailed it to a city one thousand eight hundred kilometres away, this city Red and I call home.

As I lay the fishy-smelling package on the kitchen table, Red is standing at my side, watching. Red, my best friend in this city and the one and only man in my life, asks me suspiciously where the parcel is from.

'The Village of Stone,' I answer absently.

'The Village of Stone?' The words seem to perplex Red, as if he were hearing the abstruse syllables of some remote antiquity.

The package is heavy. When I draw the enormous eel from its wrappings and set it on the table, Red freezes in shock. The eel is eerily lifelike. With its monstrous tail protruding upwards, it looks poised to swim away from us at any moment.

And in an instant, the salt scent of the East China Sea and the smell of a Village of Stone typhoon come rushing back to me, as if from the body of the eel. Synapses connect, the floodgates are thrown open, the torrents of memory unleashed. They rush through the tunnels of the past, threatening to flood the earth and blot out the sky.

I spent the first fifteen years of my life in the Village of Stone, but I have left it far behind me. I now live one thousand eight hundred kilometres away, with a man who knows nothing about my past, in a city as diametrically opposed to the Village of Stone as any place could possibly be. It has been years since I corresponded with anyone in the village, and yet now I find myself thinking about it, about the things that happened there and the people who lived there – those whose lives I passed through and whose lives passed through me.

Had it not been for that parcel of dried, salted eel sent from a faraway place, I would never have started to remember those events, all the things that happened in the Village of Stone.

That was how the memories began.

2

Let me close the door to the past for a moment, while I explain a bit about the present.

Red and I live together in the enormous, parched megalopolis that is Beijing. I'm twenty-eight and Red is twenty-nine, just a few days shy of his thirtieth birthday. Confucius said that thirty was the age at which a person should settle down, but Red and I have never had the sense of being truly settled, not in a city like this. I suppose we're at the age when people start to become sensitive about the loss of their youth, but I haven't noticed anything particularly different about being twenty-eight. Twenty-eight is just old enough to be past the ignorance of youth, yet it's still a good long way from being octogenarian. The only thing about being twenty-eight that holds any significance for me is that Mazu Niangniang, the Sea Goddess, was twenty-eight when she died. Of course, people in the Village of Stone never said that she died; they said that she 'ascended straight to heaven' and became an immortal. There wasn't a fisherman or woman in the village who didn't worship her memory. During her lifetime, Mazu Niangniang was a wise woman said to be able to predict bad weather and even rescue ships lost at sea during typhoons. When she died of an illness at the age of twenty-eight, she left in her wake a whole string of temples dedicated to her memory, temples that wafted incense smoke over the rocky, typhoon-swept promontory of the Village of Stone. And now here I am too at the age of twenty-eight, still alive and well – although I'm not sure I could be considered completely well, for I often live in fear. Fear of what, I'm not quite certain. I doubt that Mazu Niangniang ever knew fear. Maybe that's why she was able to show so much love and concern for others. As for me, I've always been one to look out for myself.

I work at a video rental shop in the north part of Beijing, up in the Haidian District on a street near University Road. It's a tiny little shop, squeezed in behind a row of huge poplars. These are the same poplars that, each spring, release millions of fluffy white seed-bearing pods that float through the sky like filthy balls of airborne cotton wool. To the left of the video rental shop is a pharmacy specialising in those kinds of medicines, toys and tonics euphemistically called 'adult items'. To the right is a shop selling brightly coloured children's clothing made by some minor manufacturer. Our three shops manage to coexist quite nicely, because none of us could ever steal the others' clientele. Although our shops are small and inconspicuous, not much more than tiny specks on the map, this city needs us, in much the same way that we need this city.

I work part time for the owner of the video shop. The shop is only twelve metres square, and the walls are covered with posters of film stars such as Jackie Chan, Tom Cruise and Julia Roberts and advertisements for films from America and Hong Kong. It's my job to rent out the tapes, so I'm behind the tiny counter every day, helping customers find the video they're looking for, ringing up sales and sneaking peeks at the latest movies. The job is a bit monotonous, but I'm happy that I can watch movies while I work and I earn enough to pay our rent. Red has just quit another job, which is probably just as well because he hates working anyway. Red says that jobs are idiotic. Fortunately, he has parents who help him out financially. When all is said and done, Red's decent, although it's hard to say how long we'll be together.

Red and I are like a pair of hermit crabs encased in a huge high-rise building. There are twenty-five storeys in our building, but we live on the ground floor. Sometimes, when we're lying in bed, nestled under the covers, it feels as if our bodies are becoming heavier, more oppressive, much harder to move around. This could have something to do with the twenty-four storeys overhead, the combined gravitational weight of thousands of our fellow residents bearing down upon us. Actually, rather than say we're like hermit crabs, it would probably be more fitting to say that we envy hermit crabs their lifestyle, for they live their lives in a portable shell. Hermit crabs can crawl out from under their shells any time they please and move into a new and more fitting shell, unlike Red and me.

And so the two of us live together in this ground-floor flat like hermits, clinging to each other as if our lives depended on it, silently reading our books and sleeping away the hours like two elderly people who know they haven't got much time left for this world. We've never tried to keep a cat, much less a dog, although we once had several potted plants that we thought might be flowering plants. We never did find out, though, because the identical twenty-five-storey high-rise opposite ours blocked most of the sunlight from our flat. In other words, if those pathetic little potted plants wanted to get any sunlight at all, they had to stretch themselves out to their full length and try to absorb all the light they could during the brief period of morning sunshine which lasted from exactly 8.00 to 8.45 a.m. If they missed those precious forty-five minutes of wan, indirect sunlight, they had to wait and try to make it up when the sun appeared for another forty-five minutes between 4.00 to 4.45 p.m. Of course, they also had to hope that their owners had remembered to remove the clothes they had hung out to dry, and all of the various and sundry other objects blocking their sunshine. If we had forgotten to clear a path, the plants were cruelly deprived of their rightful daily allowance of sunlight. For this reason, the plants succumbed to an early and perhaps fated death a mere six months after we began raising them.

At one time, we also had a pair of pop-eyed goldfish named after two of the characters in the Japanese television drama *Tokyo Love Story*, Kanji Nagao and Rika Akana. We put Kanji and

Rika together in a large green glass tank by the window, in the hope that they would carry on in the spirit of that immortal romance. However, when we realised that the process of raising goldfish mainly involved weekly trips to the market to buy replacement Kanjis and Rikas, we could not bring ourselves to condemn any more new life forms to that watery green tank. The fish tank still occupies the same space on the window sill, although it is now a much more dried-up shade of green. The romance of Kanji and Rika is but an empty memory. And so it is that the only living creatures in our gloomy ground-floor flat these days, besides the cockroaches that can occasionally be seen crawling across the floor, are Red and me.

Of course, there are the other occupants of the high-rise, who seem to spend each and every minute of each and every day cooking and chopping, fucking and fighting, flushing and showering, hammering and drilling, alternately spanking and doting on children, doing aerobics and playing mah-jong, from morning to night, weekdays, weekends and holidays. It feels as if the sheer vitality of their everyday lives, the accumulated heartiness of their quotidian existence is piling up layer upon layer above us, expanding to fill all twenty-five storeys of our building. They press down upon our drab ground-floor lives in much the same way that my childhood memories have started to bear down upon my otherwise placid existence. Sometimes I try to talk to Red about the Village of Stone, but I realise that Red really knows very little about me. The whole time we've been together, neither my feelings nor my past have figured very prominently in his life. Red and I have different lifelines; our blood runs separately. Each night our flesh may intertwine, but our memories, whether by day or by night, never mingle.

Between the tale of Red's life and the tale of my life, there is zero correlation.

Red's world, you see, is a closed circle. Not that it matters. I know that I'm a closed circle, too, and it's all I can do to find some starting point from myself, while at the same time trying to find my own terminus. There's no way I'm ever going to find my beginning or end in somebody else's circle. Two people together never add up to anything more than one person added to another. That we continue to add ourselves up in this way is the reason human beings will always be lonely.

Love is uncertain, jobs are uncertain, our future in this rented flat is uncertain. My future with Red is, if anything, even less certain.

In fact, the only thing I can say with any certainty is that I've travelled very far from that rain-drenched, typhoon-swept village by the sea. I've put a lot of distance between myself and the tiny fishing village where rooftops are covered with rocks and streets are paved with stones. I have managed to escape my childhood, the chaos and emotional turmoil of those years.

But the Village of Stone − that tiny corner of the sea that, on a map of China, appears as nothing more than a deep blue stain, with no air or shipping routes to link it with anywhere else − still exerts a strange sort of pull on me. Like a recurring dream that appears each and every midnight, or some profound and inescapable homesickness, I somehow find myself remaining loyal to its memory. I think of it at odd and unexpected moments: as I am walking through the city, listening to buses making their slow stops at deserted stations, or evenings after work, as I am in the kitchen lighting the burner and starting to make dinner, or mornings just after rising, as I am taking the top from the toothpaste tube and getting ready to brush my teeth. The memories come unbidden, like the tides of my childhood village, waters surging out of nowhere to inundate us up to our knees.

3

I was seven when it happened.

That's as far back as my memory goes, to when I was seven. Before that, my memories are blurred and indistinct, like scenes glimpsed through a pane of rain-spattered glass. But so many things happened the year I was seven, things fearful and impossible to articulate, that I would always remember that year and everything that happened after it.

I was seven, then, not so young really, just old enough to understand ordinary human feelings such as warmth and kindness. But actually, I knew that human feelings ran both hot and cold, because I had seen a lot more things than most children my age. For a child of seven, I must have appeared unusually aloof. I had never known my parents, never really had a mother or a father. My grandmother told me that my mother had given birth to me in a rowing boat. It was a difficult birth, and by the time the little boat reached shore, my mother had already died from loss of blood. Why she had taken a boat out to sea, and whether anyone was with her, my grandmother never said. Of course, I have no memory of these events. As for my father, he wasn't even there to witness them. He had fled the village before my birth to escape the fisherman's life. While he was gone the villagers branded him a 'Capitalist Roader' for his bourgeois views. This was during the Cultural Revolution, and had he returned to the village, he would have been imprisoned.

After I was born, my grandfather named me Coral, a name connected with the sea. The Chinese characters in my name mean 'red coral'. Though I've seen white coral and green coral many times, I've never actually encountered red coral. I think the red must be my mother's blood, the blood that stained the planks of the rowing boat. My grandfather also gave me a nickname, 'Little Dog'. Dog is a good nickname, a lucky name. My grandfather told me that there were more than ten children in the village nicknamed Dog; the conventional wisdom being that the worse-sounding your nickname, the less likely it was that the Sea Demon would want to carry you off. And it's true – the worst-sounding nicknames are always the luckiest. Every year during typhoon season, when the Sea Demon emerged from the ocean to carry off children playing on the shore, it was always the kids with the nice-sounding names who got taken away. After all, who in their right mind would want to take a child nicknamed Dog, or even worse, Leper?

The Village of Stone was my entire world, my fortress without windows, a place where they had dug my grave almost as soon as I was born. The villagers buried their dead on the far side of the craggy hill that stood behind the village and screened it from the world beyond. As soon as a person was born, their relatives would consult a Feng Shui practitioner to select a gravesite with an auspicious location and direction. When the site was chosen, the family would erect a tombstone bearing the newborn's name to ensure that nobody else could claim the gravesite later. How could a person bear to leave the place that had set aside a gravesite just for her the moment she was born? As a child, I didn't imagine I'd ever flee the Village of Stone, not ever.

Of course, at the age of seven, I didn't yet know the word 'flee', nor had I ever stopped to consider the concept of fleeing. I didn't miss the word, just as I had never missed my parents. You can't miss something you've never had. It was as if my parents had never existed, as if I had just spontaneously materialised in this world.

Actually, I wasn't at all like a piece of red coral. I was more like a tiny pebble that had been flung up from the sea and fallen into one of the cracks between the cobblestones, to be trampled on by passing feet. Every day the fishermen, with their fishing nets and floaters in tow, would walk through the cobblestone alleys in their waterproof boots, and the fishermen's wives would step over and around the shallow, circular bamboo baskets they used for drying shrimps. They would leave the cobblestones drenched. Then, at noon, the sun would emerge to evaporate the brackish water from the stones, so that soon, all the cobblestones were bleached a pure white and covered with a fine crust of dried sea salt. The house I grew up in was along one of those cobblestone alleyways skirting the sea. I was nothing more than a tiny stone – crusted in salt, silent, unnoticed and insignificant.

The little lane on which we lived stretched from my grandmother's doorstep all the way to the muddy roar of the sea. The cove near our house had once been a hideout for Japanese pirates, who would occasionally come up into the village to rape, loot, pillage and wreak general mayhem on the villagers. For this reason, our lane was known as 'Pirate's Alley'.

When I was seven, I would go out every day during the typhoon season, to stand idly at the end of Pirate's Alley and stare at the sea. The sea in the Village of Stone is rarely blue; in fact, the true colour of the sea is yellow-brown, the colour of soil, or a soil-coloured banner. I would stand and watch the typhoon winds churning the ocean into waves, not unlike a fisherman's wife who waits year after year for her husband to return from the sea. The rough winds buffeted me until my skin, my hair, my eyes, even my fingernails took on the colour of the sea. I was a small, soil-coloured person. My entire body was the colour of dirt. The sea was my only friend, my constant, mysterious and awe-inspiring companion. Each day I would walk down the beach and wade into the sea. The sea was unusually pungent, and tasted strongly of salt. With each cresting wave, I was immersed in the sea to my very marrow.

All my impressions of the Village of Stone begin with that cruel, muddy sea. The sound of the sea, the colour of the sea, its volume and surface area, its four seasons, its penchant for swallowing boats whole; the Sea Demon who gobbled up children from the shore during typhoon season, and the women who stood on the shore wailing for their lost men. At seven, the sea was something to be feared, something to be worshipped.

'The only thing separating a sea scavenger from the Sea Demon is three inches of wooden plank.'

Our next-door neighbour, the father of my best friend and the captain of his own fishing boat, used to say this often.

That's what the fishermen and women of the village called themselves, 'sea scavengers'. They relied on the sea, or whatever they could beg, borrow or scavenge from the sea, to provide them with a living, and that's how the name came about.

Our next-door neighbour was a sea scavenger himself, with his own boat and crew. Everyone in the village called him 'The Captain'. The Captain's skin was the colour of brass, and I thought he was the bravest of all the sea scavengers in the village. He once caught a shark, and everyone in the village came to have some of his shark cartilage soup. You are what you eat, as the saying goes. People in the village said that shark cartilage soup strengthened your bones.

At least, that's what the Captain always said. The Captain was always saying things like that.

I was often to be found by the Captain's side in those days, and whenever a damaged boat came in from the sea, he would turn to me and say:

'You know, Little Dog, the only thing separating a sea scavenger from the Sea Demon is three inches of wooden plank. You know that, don't you, Little Dog?'

The sea was all the Village of Stone had, the only nature it possessed. The village was built on a peninsula with no rivers, lakes or farmland, just the craggy, desolate mountain behind it that sloped down to the sea. The inhabitants of the Village of Stone built their houses, row upon row of them, on the lower slopes of the mountain, so that all the streets were at a sharp incline. This was partly to protect the houses from the tide, but more importantly, to prevent them from being swept away by the frequent typhoons.

To help withstand the fierce typhoon winds, every year my grandmother and all the other villagers would climb on top of their houses to pile stones onto the black tile rooftops. We children were given the task of climbing the hill to collect stones. The more stones you could pile onto a rooftop, the less likely that it would be ripped off and carried away by the typhoons – assuming, of course, the weight of the stones themselves didn't make the roof collapse first. And so the village was truly transformed into a Village of Stone: the houses were built from boulders found around the peninsula, the streets were paved with smaller pebbles, and even the rooftops were covered with piles of stones. No matter how you looked upon the village – from the ground, from the hillside, even from the sky above – it really was a village constructed entirely of stone.

Nor was there even any soil in the village, for the constant storms that lashed the peninsula during typhoon season had eroded the ground bit by bit, until all the remaining topsoil had been washed away. The typhoons and rainstorms carried away everything they could – all the smallest, feeblest bits of matter, weeds and roots and seeds, dandelions growing up through the cracks in the walls – until the only things remaining were the large chunks of rock.

Every year during the typhoons, the houses of the village were flooded and, after the storms had subsided, it was not unusual to find lone slippers and errant chopsticks bobbing up and down in pools of water. I remember once finding some golden incense burners floating around, along with a white statue of Guanyin, the Buddhist Goddess of Mercy, now rendered every bit as powerless as me, a mere child. Wading through water well past my knees, I finally caught sight of some grown-ups paddling towards me, and I began to cry and shout. At that moment, though, the grown-ups noticed the statue floating away and, horrified, hurried to fish it out of the water. Only then did they take me in their arms and carry me home to safety.

I can't remember now whether or not the Village of Stone had any trees. It seems to me that it was a place without any vegetation at all. It stands to reason that there must have been something, but the only green I can remember is the green of the fishing nets spread out on the shore. The nets looked just like green dragons sprawled out along the beach, knotted strands of green nylon twisting and tangling, coiling around the women as they worked, repairing the nets. There were always children scampering around, and although they were forever tripping and falling over the nets, they never cried. In fact, they could often be found sleeping peacefully, snuggled into thick piles of fishing nets.

On the days the fishermen weren't at sea, they would spread the green fishing nets out in the courtyards of their houses to dry in the sun. That's right . . . the courtyards. Now I remember, there was greenery in the courtyards. In the winter, there were the green leaves of the narcissus plants with their long stalks. The villagers planted the narcissus in large nautilus shells filled with earth. I remember the rows of nautilus shells that lined the window sills of the houses during winter, each of the plants a profusion of green leaves and yellow flowers. All winter those narcissus plants would perch on the window sills like tiny statues of Guanyin. But the minute spring arrived, bringing with it the southerly winds, every narcissus would wither overnight. It was as if someone in the village had blown a whistle, sending some signal to the plants that caused their yellow flowers to wither en masse.

Nor did I ever encounter spring in the Village of Stone. Spring? What was spring? I remember springtime only as the season that brought southerly winds and rainstorms gusting into the village. The hot, wet southerlies blew from the surface of the ocean, seeping into every last house of the Village of Stone, making the walls so damp they seemed to be perspiring. The wind brought with it a dripping heaviness that wound itself around your body, penetrating your hair, your skin, your every pore. It was like beeswax, gluing the inhabitants of the village to that sheet of dirt-coloured ocean. Even on days when the skies were clear as far as the eye could see and sunshine reflected from the surface of that boundless sea, you could feel the damp gusts of wind on your skin and know that the rain was not far off.

When I was seven years old, I would stand at the end of Pirate's Alley, watching the tide recede from the shoreline to reveal the jagged edges of reef, gazing at the fishermen's wives, who sat along the beach and chattered as they wove their fishing nets, white gardenias tucked into their hair. I see now that my memory has been playing tricks on me because those white gardenias also grew in the courtyards. That tiny, cloyingly fragrant flower that the fishermen's wives would weave into their shiny coils of hair somehow managed to survive the storms, its fine white petals bursting into bloom as the typhoons raged all around. I remember the plants clearly now, sprouting from cracked pottery jars in the fishermen's courtyards. Sometimes people would plant the gardenias in rusty chamber pots that had belonged to some-body's ageing father or grandfather and been recycled after he died. Just before autumn, the gardenia flowers would start to wither up and bear fruit, a small yellow fruit that the fisher-women plucked from the plants to grind with a mortar and pestle into a sort of dye. The more aesthetically inclined village women would dye their plain white cotton shirts in a basin filled with the fragrant dye. Afterwards, they could be seen proudly sporting these bright yellow shirts through the streets.

And there is another fragrance wafting through my memo-ries of the Village of Stone. How could I have forgotten the jasmine trees next to the primary school where we all went when we were eight? The fragrant white jasmine blossomed all over the small playground, suffusing it with the spirit of jasmine, turning it into an expanse of snow-white flowers. It got so that it became impossible to play with a skipping rope or run around because of the branches of jasmine. At the morning flag cere-mony, the fragrant blossoms even obscured the red flag that was hoisted up in the playground. As we raised our hands over our heads in salute, we would search around for the flag that we were supposed to be saluting, only to find that it had been swallowed up by an expanse of jasmine. Later, when the fragrance of jasmine became too overpowering, the students would become giddy with the scent, some of them allergic and sneezing, others fighting and stumbling beneath the branches. The scent would seep out of the schoolyard and waft through the entire village. Sometimes the village women would come to break off large branches and take them home to dry in the sun. When the flowers had dried, the women would tuck them into the family's bedding and storage chests during the rainy season.

'The sea is meant to be eaten,' my grandfather used to say. He claimed that everything in the sea was edible: sea urchins, sea cucumbers, starfish, algae, kelp, even rocks from the reef, which he said could be sucked. My grandfather was fiercely adamant about this.

'Even the reef can be sucked and eaten.' I would imitate my grandfather as I said this, sounding as fiercely adamant as he.

Every day, the tide would recede to reveal the black reef, covered with a layer of lichen green. Underneath the reef were clumps of oysters, so well camouflaged in their slate-grey shells that they were easily mistaken for the pointed edges of the reef. In the crevices between the rocks you could see dark-blue mussel shells, and inside these, the fleshy, salmon-pink mussels that we called 'sea vermilions'. We would sometimes also find a particularly disgusting type of sea organism in amongst the rocks – slippery, luridly coloured creatures with long protuberant heads that adhered to the surface of the rocks and, when you cut or bit into them, oozed a thick, yellowish fluid. The villagers called them 'sea pricks' and said they looked exactly like a certain part of a man's body. Whenever someone raised the subject of the sea pricks – usually when the grown-ups had been sitting around drinking, telling stories and eating salted peanuts – everyone would laugh.

One of the men would say: 'I'll be damned if I can sleep at night lately.'

And another would say: 'Can't sleep at night? Well, just boil yourself up some of them sea pricks. They'll give you strength.'

And the man who couldn't sleep at night would answer: 'Who needs more strength? I'd get even less sleep then!'

Then someone else would shout: 'If you had more strength, you could make it with your wife! Then you'd sleep just fine!'

At this, everyone would burst into riotous laughter, knock back a few more shots of sorghum whisky, and before long, the salted peanuts would be gone.

The men used boil the sea pricks into a kind of broth, to which they would add ginger to make a thick, muddy-looking soup. It was said to be a very good tonic – even my grand-mother said so. But of course, she never made the soup for me.

The coarseness of life in the Village of Stone derived from the sea. From the time I was small, I knew the ocean to be the most profound of things; she gave birth to everything, devoured everything. We lived and died by her. The brave fishermen who ventured out into her belly sometimes returned with their plunder; sometimes they didn't return at all. In the same way, many of the fishing boats and nets that the fishermen dragged along the coast ended up buried at sea. To me, the sea was more terrifying than death.

Every day, I would stand on the beach watching the tide recede, waiting for the fishing boats to return. I never knew how the horde of boats knew to come in at the same time; whether they'd arranged the time in advance, or whether they'd made the decision based on the position of the sun in the sky. At any rate, the boats would always come in to shore together, the sound of their motors preceding them. The sound drew everyone in the village – old folk, children and fishermen's wives – out of their houses and onto the foaming shore to wait for the boats.

The oil from the boat engines polluted the beach and covered the surface of the harbour with an oily film, creating whorls of rainbow-coloured oil slicks. The oil even made its way into the bodies of the fish that swam in these waters. As the fishermen turned off their engines for the approach to port, you could see the piles of fish stacked on the decks of the fishing boats: mountains of shimmering fish, transparent shrimp, black mussels and sea eels. The fishing boats coming home with their catch were entirely different from the fishing boats that had set out empty-handed early one morning. They were coming home with a bellyful.

As the setting sun threw into relief the silhouettes of the fishermen and their fishing boats, the fishermen's wives, who had spent many long days and nights awaiting the return of their men from the sea, excitedly called out their husbands' names. With children in tow, the women rushed towards their respective boats. It was at times like these that I felt the loneliest, because I knew that my own father wouldn't be on any of those fishing boats. Nor was my mother one of the women sitting on the shore, weaving rings of white gardenia or making fishing nets. As for my grandfather, he had retired from the sea long ago and was now just an old man who sold cigarettes in the street. My grandmother had been born on the 'outside' and so would always be considered an outsider in the Village of Stone. This vast and endless ocean, this stretch of sandy beach, the triumphant return of the fishermen with their bounty, the exultant welcome of the families – this was a scene in which I, as a lone seven-year-old, had absolutely no part.

After the drama of triumphant return had been played out, the beach lay silent, littered with the dead bodies of the fish and shrimp that had been discarded by the fishmongers. The sea was completely empty now; no sails skimming across its surface, nobody waiting along its shores, just the sea breezes and the distant shouts of women calling their children home to dinner. Their voices echoed from the hillside, calling out their children's names: Boy Waiting, Number Three, Dee Fu, Dee Cee. These were the names of my childhood playmates.

Boy Waiting was the seventh in a line of consecutive baby

girls born to our next-door neighbour the Captain and his wife. Her parents were very anxious for a son, so they named their daughter 'Boy Waiting' to indicate that they were still waiting for a boy. This name, they hoped, would hasten the birth of a son. Boy Waiting had an older sister named Golden Phoenix, the effective leader of that family of girls. I thought Golden Phoenix was the most beautiful girl in the whole Village of Stone. Golden Phoenix loved to sing the traditional local opera, and was as graceful and willowy as a cherry tree. With her tiny mouth and lovely long hair she looked like one of the beautiful actresses who played the role of Lin Meimei in the famous tragic love story, *Dream of Red Mansions*. Boy Waiting, unfortunately, resembled me much more than she did her sister. Both of us were tomboys through and through, unattractive children with dark skin and unruly hair, and runny noses that we were constantly wiping on our sleeves. Most people viewed the two of us as repulsive little urchins.

As for Number Three, she was a little girl with an unpleasantly swollen right cheek. When she was small, she had eaten some kind of wild fruit growing on the slopes of the mountain. The very same day, she came down with a high fever and became so ill that she could hardly breathe. In time, the fever subsided, but the right side of her face remained swollen. Her parents took her to the village clinic, where the doctors gave her acupuncture, inserting the needles directly into her cheek, but they weren't able to get rid of the swelling. And so Number Three, who had always been a cute little child, was suddenly transformed into an ugly little girl with a swollen right cheek.

My other playmates were two brothers, Dee Fu and Dee Cee, whom my grandmother called my 'nephews'. Dee Fu and Dee Cee were older than me, so I have no idea why they called me their auntie. My grandmother, who still believed in things like family rank and pedigree, didn't seem to think it at all unusual that I had become an auntie to boys from a 'lesser' family. Dee Fu and Dee Cee were wild boys who, by the ages of three and four, were already swimming in the ocean and catching mudskippers with their bare hands. I think they thought me a very strange auntie, something of a village freak. Because I had never had any parents, it was as if I were some creature who had leaped up from the stones that paved Pirate's Alley.

In among the echoes of the mothers calling their children home, I could hear my grandmother's voice calling to me. 'Little Dog, Little Dog . . . get yourself home to eat!'

My grandmother's voice was both shrill and mournful. It lingered like a long whistle, careening through the hills and echoing across the ocean. Like an enormous net dropped from the sky to cover both the land and the sea, there was no escaping it. I would wait for the echoes of her voice to subside, then burrow out from whatever pile of rocks or outcropping of reef I had been hiding in. As I emerged, I could see the setting sun turning the golden sea to flame, burning into it a brilliant red that was soon extinguished, as the sea and sky went ashen grey.

Barefoot, I clambered back onto the beach, leaving behind me the sea at its saddest and most mournful time of day, and began making my way towards my grandmother's voice.

As I ascended solid ground and crossed the cobblestones of Pirate's Alley, I knew exactly what would be waiting for me in the stone house I called home. Sitting on the old-fashioned wooden table would be the same meal that I ate three times a day, morning, noon and night: a bowl of sweet potato gruel garnished with a pungent paste of pickled fish.

4

In the summer, the city of Beijing is like a piping-hot baked tomato. You can scarcely bear to touch anything lest your touch release the scalding liquid inside. Then there are the sounds of the city, noises of every decibel: taxi drivers cursing each other, cries of 'Every item only ten yuan!' and 'Evening news . . . get your evening news!' and the non-stop ding-a-ling of bicycle bells. The sounds only serve to raise the temperature even higher, turning the city into a gigantic convection oven from which the heat never dissipates.

I return home from work early to find Red in bed, reading a book. Lying there perfectly still, not moving a single muscle, as if he were loath to deplete any more physical energy than absolutely necessary, he looks a bit like a reclining Buddha. I peel off my sticky clothes and lie down next to him. With all the windows closed and the air conditioner hard at work above our heads, the room is freezing. The sweat from my body slowly evaporates. The room temperature has dropped to twelve degrees, the temperature of a cold winter's day, but still we allow the air conditioner to continue huffing its frigid air into the room. Both of us are far too lazy to get up and turn it off, just as we are too lazy to try to warm up our bodies, from which the heat is steadily slipping away. We lie in bed holding hands and staring up at the ceiling, as if there were some fascinating long-running television drama being projected on the twenty-four storeys above.

I gaze around the room at our few sad pieces of furniture. Beneath the window stand a rapidly unravelling rattan chair and a battered desk on whose surface someone has drawn the outlines of a 'go' board in ballpoint pen. Upon the desk is perched an old computer, an unattractive desk-lamp and a collection of Red's reference books. Besides the two large wardrobes we bought at a used furniture market, the only other thing in the room is our Peony-brand television set. Piled next to it is a stack of video cassettes intended for rental in the shop. When we have finished watching them, I will quietly sneak them back onto the shelves. The bed beneath us is just a mattress lying on the bare floor. People say that when you're nearing thirty, you ought at least to have a proper bed, but since we still live in a rented flat, investing in a bed seems a bit pointless.

The only spot of brightness in our room is the curtains. They are a fiery red, the colour we imagine the sun might be, if only we could see it. Managing to catch a glimpse of actual sunlight in our flat is no easy task. By the time we wake in the morning, the sun has already passed us by. And though we may hurry through the door after work each evening, rush to set down our groceries and walk over towards the window, we always find ourselves a few seconds too late to catch its last rays.

The main room of our flat is a combination bedroom/living room. The only other rooms are the kitchen and bathroom, which connect onto the main room, and a tiny entrance hall. Taken as a whole, the place seems old. The type of old that is devoid of memory, a complete void, the sort of old that holds no hope of progress.

Nothing can ever be captured. The only thing that never seems to resist capture is the male body. Red's body.

Once more, I feel my temperature starting to rise. I roll over languidly and begin to stroke Red's naked body.

I'm wet again. I spread Red's fingers, gently, and put them inside me.

'You're hot,' he tells me. 'Your body temperature is always higher than mine.'

'That's because I'm a torrid zone.'

'Torrid zone, eh? I guess that makes me the temperate zone.'

'That's right. You never burn too hot.'

I ask Red if he knows the difference between the torrid zone and the temperate zone.

'The torrid zone and the temperate zone? Um . . . they're separated by the subtropical zone?'

'Wrong. The difference is, it hardly ever rains in the temperate zone. But in the torrid zone, it rains all the time.'

'No wonder it's always so wet . . .' Red and I smile at each other. His fingers are already finding the wetness inside me.

On the wall opposite our bed is an enormous poster from the Greek film *Ulysses' Gaze*, from which a black-clad Harvey Keitel stares down at us day and night. The poster is one I pilfered from the video store. With the exception of one extremely melancholy-looking middle-aged man in glasses, I never saw anyone rent the film.

When Red and I make love in this room surrounded on all four sides by high-rise buildings, on this bed separated from the basement by just a thin slab of concrete, I can feel Harvey Keitel watching us from the poster. There is something in his expression that calls to mind a father distastefully observing his daughter in a tryst with her lover, and it always makes me uncomfortable.

'You're like quicksand,' Red tells me. 'I sink right in and can't seem to get out.'

I can feel his fingers moving deeper inside me. 'That's your middle finger, isn't it?'

He seems surprised. 'How did you know?'

'I can tell from the length.'

'Oh,' he smiles, 'so now you love my middle finger more than you love me?'

I smile as Red sits up in bed and gropes around for a packet of cigarettes and a lighter. He lights a cigarette and inhales deeply.

The room is very quiet now. I lie in bed and watch Red

smoke. Torrid woman and temperate man definitely present two very different attitudes to the world. Red, as temperate man, is almost always cool and collected.

'I like the way you look when you smoke.'

'What else do you like about me?'

'I like it when you're peaceful.'

'And?'

'And when you're playing Frisbee.'

At this, a look of slight pain passes over Red's features.

'Hm . . . so you like my middle finger, you like me when I'm peaceful and you like me when I'm playing Frisbee. But none of those things are really me. They're just extensions of me.'

'So what's the *real* you?'

'I . . .' Red thinks for a moment, 'I don't really know.'

'But you must know who you are, right? A hero, a nobody, a gentleman, a Mister Average, a traditionalist, a hopeless romantic, a loser? Which one are you?'

Red looks at me as he exhales. 'You know, girl, you really have seen too many movies.'

'I work in a video rental shop. Watching movies is my job.'

'It's just that sometimes I feel like everything you say to me is dialogue from some movie.'

I have no answer for this.

Perhaps because our daily lives are so depressing, Red is captivated by the game of Frisbee, that flat white plastic disc he so loves to send spinning through the air. Red has a wide variety of Frisbee throws in his repertoire. He can throw clockwise or anticlockwise, backhanded or forehanded, with a flick of his thumb and even with the back of his hand. Not only has he mastered these and all the basic catches – the left-handed catch, the 'pinch' catch, the low catch and others – but he has also invented a number of unusual moves of his own, most of which he has yet to find names for. Red can play all day and never let the Frisbee touch the ground. He loves the game so much that sometimes he even plays by himself. He'll stake out an open stretch of grass or an empty concrete rooftop, stand in one spot, and hurl the Frisbee in a perfect three hundred and sixty degree arc so that it flies right back to him. Red says that he loves the feeling of knowing that even when the Frisbee is flying through the air, it is still under his complete control. Frisbee is freestyle yet elegant, peaceful and safe, and that is why Red loves it so much.

I sometimes think Red wishes he *were* a Frisbee. Every day he sees people getting into the lift and ascending to his rooftop, people who are moving up in the world, while he himself remains stuck on the ground floor. If Red does believe in an afterlife, he probably wishes he could come back as a Frisbee.

Although Red is not the type to complain about his lot in life, his one gripe is that neither the Olympics nor the Asian Games recognises Frisbee as an official event, which means he is deprived of his chance to be World Frisbee Grand Champion. The people Red detests most are those he considers the 'narrow interpretationists' of the sports world, who think of Frisbee as nothing more than a child's game and refuse to take it seriously as a sport. Red, on the other hand, believes that Frisbee is uniquely suited to be the universal sport. That's right, the universal sport. A simple game that can be played anywhere, any time, in any country, by rich or poor, man or woman, heavyweight or feather-weight; a sport that helps to improve reflexes, speed, endurance, control, coordination and imagination, thereby creating an environ-ment of freedom for each and every player.

Here in Beijing, Red has devised a new game of Frisbee. It is similar to American-style football in that the players must rely on speed and agility to prevent the other team from making a goal in their end zone, but each team has only seven players and the Frisbee is never allowed to touch the ground. Red is planning a city-wide Frisbee tournament that will bring people from different countries, professions and walks of life together onto the same playing field to play Frisbee according to Red's strict set of rules. Red, the man now lying so quietly by my side, remains unshaken in his belief that there will come a day when Frisbee is finally recognised as an official Olympic event. When that day comes, Red is certain that he will become the World Frisbee Grand Champion, assuming he is still young enough to hold the title. And if by chance he is too old, well, at least he will be acknowledged as the senior statesman of the international sport of Frisbee. Red is, quite simply, a Frisbee god. No, not a Frisbee god: a Frisbee sage.

The problem is that, every time Red tosses me the Frisbee, I can never quite manage to catch it. And if you can't even hold on to a Frisbee, what makes you think you can hold on to another person?

We lie in bed silently, completely still, holding hands, huddled under blankets against the air conditioned chill of a summer's day, as the sky outside grows steadily darker. After a while, Red seems to fall asleep and in his slumber releases my hand. As our physical bodies move apart, Red's inner world moves farther and farther away from me. Already I cannot begin to fathom what thoughts must fill his dreams. Perhaps he has already entered into his own Frisbee dream world, a place with green grass and blue skies, God's own backyard. Once again I find myself alone. And, as I lie in bed, my body and my spirit move away from Red and towards the vast sea and narrow alleyways of the Village of Stone and all the people I knew there.

5

My grandmother and grandfather lived at 13 Pirate's Alley, in a three-storey stone house facing onto the street. In fact, the street number wasn't there when I was little. I must have been about thirteen years old when the village authorities, responding to requests from frustrated employees of the local post office, finally decided to install metal street number signs on each of the houses in the village. Formerly, the sole person in charge of incoming and outgoing mail was an elderly postmaster who could recite by rote the names and locations of each and every resident in the village. When the old postmaster died, two younger men were assigned to take over his duties, but because they were unfamiliar with the layout of the village, half of the incoming post ended up being delivered incorrectly. The two young postmen finally appealed to local government officials, who decided that every lane would be assigned an official name and every house a number. In order to do this, they convened a meeting of older village residents to discuss possible street names. And so the agreed-upon names – Pirate Slayer Road, Marshy Lane, Dogfish Alley – were painted in red calligraphy on stone markers at the end of each lane. I was told that each of the names had a story behind it, some tale associated with the fight against Japanese sea pirates or other invaders, and the earliest origins of the Village of Stone.

When the time came to number the houses in our lane, we were given a metal plaque with the number thirteen, indicating that we lived in the thirteenth house from the east end of Pirate's Alley. But, during my childhood, whenever the villagers mentioned my grandfather's house, they would always refer to it as 'the house without a fisherman'. And it was true. We were one of the few families in the village who were not sea scavengers. Ours was a house without a fisherman.

Our house had quite a long history. My seafaring great-grandfather had built the house so that it would face out to sea, though none of his descendants turned out to be fishermen – not my grandfather, who had abandoned his boat to sell cigarettes, not my father, who had fled the village, and certainly not myself, a young girl not even allowed on the fishing boats. With each successive generation, our family continued to renounce the sea. We must have been the most spineless family of cowards in the entire village. None of us fished and yet we still had the nerve to live in that house right beside the sea. Then again, perhaps my grandfather was right when he said, 'Life is hard enough as it is. Best to live in safety.' For fishermen, life never afforded any safety.

Our house was identical to the others in the village in that it was a sturdy little fortress with tiny windows, cramped and narrow but built to last. The adults in the village said the houses had been designed this way to repel Japanese sea pirates and other plunderers. The walls were built from greenish chunks of stone piled one upon another. None of the stones was the same shape. Some were large, some small, some rounded and some square, but they seemed to fit together perfectly. They had been brought down from the mountaintop on shoulder poles. The men who blasted the stone from the hillside came to the mountain fleeing famine in other parts of the country. The explosives they used were generally very crude and home-made, so many of them were killed in accidents. These men led a life of hardship in much the same way that the sea scavengers did. The difference was that, once these men had managed to earn some money blasting rock, they left the Village of Stone and returned to their home towns to live out their remaining days in peace.

My grandfather's second-floor room had a small window that

had been cut out of the stones in the wall. Though the window was tiny, it afforded a view of the sea. When my grandfather ate his meals, he would often stand at the tiny stone window with his bowl and gaze out to sea. Although the window was not much more than a peephole, it did admit the ocean breeze. My grandfather would stand in the breeze and stare for a long time at the churning waves of the sea. It was as if he were seeing an ocean that belonged to someone else.

One other thing about my grandmother and grandfather. They despised each other.

It had been decades since my grandparents had truly lived together. They had shared the same room until my father was born but, after that, they slept in separate rooms. In fact, they hardly spoke to one another. My grandmother had been brought into my grandfather's house at an early age, as a child-bride. Her home was a mountain village several hundred kilometres from the Village of Stone. Besides four or five date trees, a sweet potato patch and a small group of mud-walled houses it contained nothing of note. When my grandmother was twelve years old, she bundled up her few possessions in a strip of cloth and left her home, journeying east on foot for three days and three nights. By dusk on the fourth day, she had finally reached the foot of the mountains near the Village of Stone. As the smell of raw fish wafted up into the mountains and grew more pungent, my grandmother crossed through the last mountain pass, surmounted the very last peak and caught her first glimpse of the sea being turned to gold by the dazzling rays of the setting sun. Gazing at the fishing nets filled with glittering silver fish that had just been dragged onto shore, she must have believed that she would never again suffer from hunger. However, she never had the chance to live the life of a fisherman's wife she so dreamed of. My grandfather had only been at sea for a few years but had already encountered several devastating typhoons that ripped his sail, smashed his prow and eventually ran his fishing boat aground. The wreckage of his boat languished on the beach for years until he decided to sell it to a local youth looking for work. After this, my grandfather lived a safer and more carefree life ashore, selling cigarettes, alcohol, vinegar and other daily necessities, from which he managed to make a modest living and support the wife who had come to him without so much as a dowry to her name.

My grandfather had always looked down on my grandmother. He had never liked her – not on the day she arrived in his household as a child of twelve, not when she was a grown woman, not when she gave birth to my father at the age of eighteen, not when my father left the village for good, not even when she was a toothless old woman with white hair. As a child, I never understood why. I imagined all sorts of stories – a love affair with a girl in another village perhaps – but the real reasons were beyond me. My grandparents' inner feelings were a bottomless sea: cold, unfathomable, deathly still, frozen solid. Year after year, my grandmother refused to speak, as did my grandfather. Our little three-storey house was a silent, gloomy place. The only noise was the sound of doors turning on their hinges as they opened and closed. It was the sound of loneliness, the sound of unhappiness. For as long as I can remember, my grandparents had lived only within the tiny spaces of their own private hearts. Although they occasionally brushed past each other on the stairs, they never interacted. This lack of connection naturally led to a series of misunderstandings, suspicions and hateful jealousies that accumulated over the years. Stored in the separate camps of my grandparents' hearts, these grievances grew into a lasting enmity.

At seven, I was the only remaining link between those two old people. But as I found myself being pushed and pulled from one to the other, my grandparents remained completely unaware that I had taken neither side. I was like the vast ocean – immersed in my own thoughts, appearing now and again only to recede once more into the distance, living each and every day solely within my own ebb and flow.

In most of the houses facing onto our lane, the front part of the ground floor was given over to a small shop selling rice noodles, spirits or hairdressing services, while pigs were kept in the back. We, however, had nothing on the ground floor of our house except the kitchen. From its ceiling hung a dried eel that my grandmother could never quite bring herself to eat, so it hung from the rafters year after year, slowly hardening until it looked more like a museum specimen than something you would actually want to eat. The cistern used for storing water was a large porcelain vat occupying a whole corner of the kitchen. On top of the cistern was a hollow scoop, made from a small dried pumpkin, which we used for ladling water. Next to the cistern was a wood-burning stove with a set of drawers that acted as bellows. On the wall, there was a cupboard filled with dishes and utensils and, below that, two small white porcelain statues of Guanyin, the Goddess of Mercy, and Mazu Niangniang, the Sea Goddess. Next to the kitchen door was the large wooden dining table, flanked by two long, narrow benches.

Other than that, there was nothing of value on the ground floor of the house. A set of steep wooden stairs connected it with the first and second floors of the house. My grandmother lived on the first floor, my grandfather on the second. On each landing was a red lacquer chamber pot, one belonging to my grandmother, the other to my grandfather. My grandfather's chamber pot had been bequeathed to him by his parents. The red lacquer surface had faded away entirely, exposing the original wood beneath, and a high curved handle jutted from the top. My grandmother's chamber pot was newer, having been purchased as a part of her wedding trousseau. The traditional scarlet character signifying 'double happiness' was still visible on the seat; even the red lacquer on the surface of the handle was still intact. These two chamber pots served as the points demarcating my grandparents' separate worlds.

My grandmother cooked her meals on the wood-burning stove in the kitchen and my grandfather cooked his meals on a small single-burner stove on the second floor. There was rarely anything good to eat in the kitchen. Not only was my grandmother a Buddhist who didn't believe in eating meat, she had lost all her teeth and could not chew solid food. This, combined with the fact that my grandparents kept their funds strictly separate and my grandmother was always very poor, meant that, for almost every meal, she cooked vegetable gruel or something similarly boiled into mush. This was seasoned with shrimp, crab or fish paste, which we ate on alternating days. Crab paste was made by soaking raw shelled crabs in a mixture of salt and alcohol for three days, after which the paste was ready to be eaten. As for the fish paste, it was so overpoweringly salty that a tiny pinch was enough to season two bowls of gruel. There was always a bottle of apparently endless shrimp paste perched on the dining table in the kitchen. It seemed that we had been eating that same bottle of shrimp paste for ever and yet it remained full.

Very occasionally my grandmother added some shredded fish or bits of pork to the gruel, which she would pick out with her chopsticks for me to eat, but, other than the boiled fish balls she made for holidays, these were the most sumptuous meals she prepared.

Often, as I was sitting with my grandmother at the large, wooden table, my grandfather would come home and see me sipping my gruel. He would take one look at the contents of my bowl and make a beeline for the stairs, without so much as casting a glance at my grandmother. A few minutes after he had gone upstairs, I would hear the sound of something being stir-fried and soon afterwards, the delicious smell of food would waft downstairs. I would hear my grandfather calling me: 'Little Dog! Little Dog . . .' If I didn't answer to that, he would call me by my real name, Coral. Having finished my bowl of gruel, I would glance at my grandmother. She would turn her back to me and pretend to wash the dishes, signalling that she meant me to go upstairs. And so, with my belly already full, I would climb the stairs to the second floor to eat my grandfather's cooking. My grandfather ate meat at every meal. Sometimes he would prepare a freshly caught eel or pork cooked in a clay pot, to which he added soy sauce for flavouring. His meals were delicious, and I always gobbled them down. It was as if I were a born refugee, a little soil-coloured refugee who, having starved to death in a previous life, was given twice her share in the next. Each mealtime was divided between my grandmother and grandfather, so I always ate twice. For this reason, my belly was usually swollen as round as a pumpkin. When I ate meals with my grandfather, we never spoke. The only noises were the sound of chewing or the sound of my grandmother downstairs beating a wooden fish drum as she chanted her sutras.

As I grew older, I gradually gleaned from the older residents of the Village of Stone the origins of my grandparent's falling-out. They claimed that it was mainly my grandmother's fault. The key, they told me, was that my grandmother did not know how to behave. Later, however, I realised that my grandmother's most fatal error was simply not being born in the Village of Stone.

The villagers looked down on my grandmother from the very first day she arrived in my grandfather's household. That day, as she was upstairs washing off the dirt from her long trek in a large wooden tub, her new husband's family was preparing a meal to welcome her. It was to be the first and last time that anyone cooked for her in the Village of Stone. The table was laden with all sorts of freshly caught seafood – tiny crucian sea carp, long narrow hairtail and even some freshly caught razor clams, which my grandmother, having grown up in a moun-tain village, had never seen before. Afraid to try the clams, my grandmother decided to eat the fish instead. Unfortunately, she had no inkling of the complex set of rules governing the eating of fish in the Village of Stone. For the villagers, descended from generation upon generation of fishermen, a boat was home, the sea was life itself, and fish were a symbol of every type of good or bad fortune that could possibly befall a fisherman.

On that first day, in the presence of her newly adoptive parents-in-law and a husband ten years her senior, my grandmother looked at the bones of the fish they had just picked clean and decided that it would be a good idea to turn the fish over with her chopsticks. As soon as she overturned the fish, her father-in-law, who had been the captain of a fishing boat for his entire life, became extremely agitated, as did her mother-in-law. My grandfather, who had only been at sea a short time but had already had several bad experiences, was even more furious, for the conventional wisdom of the village fishermen dictated that a fish should never be overturned at the dinner table, lest their boats capsize at sea. If a person wanted to eat the underside of a fish, he or she was supposed to use chopsticks to dig the meat out from underneath. This newly adopted daughter-in-law, raised in the mountains and ignorant of the rules for eating fish, had committed the cardinal sin: she had capsized a fish in the presence of two fishermen. The faces around the table grew stony. Had it not been a beginner's honest mistake, my grandmother would have been driven away from the table with blows and curses. As it was, my grandfather's family managed to keep their anger to themselves and refrain from cursing her outright.

In the course of a meal in the Village of Stone, however, there were many other fishermen's rules to consider. For example, it was unacceptable to poke out the eyes of a fish and eat them because the villagers painted their fishing boats to look like large fish with red eyes. The bow of each boat was painted blue, the hull black and white and the stern yellow. The red eyes painted on the side of the fishing boats symbolised a boat's 'eyes'. Removing these eyes was thought to 'blind' the boat, rendering it unable to see the catch or avoid being run aground on the reef. After capsizing the fish, my grandmother sensed the family's muffled anger and so did not dare to eat any more of the meat from the overturned fish. Instead, she modestly took a few bites of rice, removed the eyes of the fish with her chopsticks and began to eat them. My great-grandfather could stand it no longer. He ordered his twelve-year-old adoptive daughter-in-law away from the family table and into the kitchen to finish her meal alone. As for her mother-in-law, she slammed her chopsticks down and abruptly left the table. Witnessing this scene, my grandfather realised that it was already too late to return the wedding gifts and get rid of this unwelcome bride, so he refused to speak to her instead.

After that, my grandmother was permanently banished from the family's dining table. She lived most of her life consigned to the kitchen, where she stoked the fires and prepared the meals, emptied the chamber pots and shelled the shrimp, did the dusting and made the fish balls. But my grandmother was unable to keep the curse of the sea at bay for long. Soon after the dinner table incident, both my great-grandfather and my grandfather met with mishaps while at sea, mishaps that they promptly blamed on my grandmother.

My grandmother gradually came to understand the rules of the villagers, or at least was able to gain some mastery of traditional village etiquette and prohibitions. By that time, however, it was too late for my grandfather to begin liking her. She had made far too many unforgivable mistakes. For example, after she finished washing the pots and pans, she would throw the dirty water outside into the street. This was fine, because all the residents of the village were in the habit of throwing their used dishwater out into the cobbled streets. The cracks between the stones were large enough for the water to disappear quickly into the crevices. But there came a day when my grandmother threw used dishwater out into the street and onto the head of a passing fisherman. The unfortunate man, soaked to the skin, unleashed a torrent of abuse upon my grandmother. He claimed that he would never be able to set out to sea again because if he did, he was sure to meet with a typhoon that would capsize his boat. As the fisherman stood in the middle of Pirate's Alley bemoaning his cursed fate, he attracted quite a number of curious onlookers. My grandfather's house was rather unfortunately located in the middle of one of the village's main thoroughfares, so all the neighbours from one end of the street to the other heard the altercation. Within a minute, the fisherman's wife, who was even more superstitious than her husband, came running from a neighbouring lane to see what the commotion was all about. As she pushed her way through the crowd and caught sight of my grandmother, she began hurling invective, heaping curses upon my grandmother and several generations of my grandmother's ancestors.

At that very moment, my grandfather returned from the market to find a large crowd of angry villagers blocking the entrance to his house. Terribly humiliated by the whole scene, my grandfather snatched up a broom from the doorway and, in full view of the crowd, began to beat my grandmother about the head. This seemed to placate public anger somewhat, but there was still compensation to be made. In order to dispel the terrible curse that my grandmother had wrought on that poor fisherman, not to mention eight generations of his descendants, simply by pouring water on his head, my grandfather had no choice but to offer the man a bottle of his finest liquor and a packet of expensive cigarettes. With this token of apology and compensation, the matter was finally laid to rest.

I think that must have been the first time my grandfather beat my grandmother in public. Afterwards, my grandmother refused to speak, nursing her grievances in silence. She became furtive and timid, as if she lived in fear of making another mistake. Her silence and submissiveness, however, only served to fuel my grandfather's hatred towards her.

It seems to me, though, that my grandmother's true enemy was not my grandfather, but the entire Village of Stone, where she would always be an outsider. While the other village women sat on the beach weaving fishing nets and waiting for their men to return with the catch, my grandmother stood alone in the surf. She had no real connection with that ocean. None of those returning fishing boats held any spoils for her, or any catch, or any long-awaited man. Ostracised by the village women and the fishermen, who avoided her like the plague, my grandmother had nothing to do with the returning boats, the typhoons at sea or the incense smoke that filled the temple of the Sea Goddess. The Village of Stone and the sea of the Village of Stone had earned my grandmother's lifelong enmity.

6

After each meal shared with my grandparents, I would recede from their house and into my own hidden world. That world was my darkness, my midnight, my secret hell – and it was under the absolute control of the village mute.

The mute was not old. He had short, black hair, a strong build and seemed to be in his late thirties or early forties. He never dressed like the village fishermen, with their shirts of coarse blue cloth and baggy silken trousers tied around the ankles to keep out the sea winds and moisture. All year round, he could be seen wearing the same very proper grey Mao suit. The mute was not a sea scavenger and, like most of the men in the village who did not fish, was considered a bit odd. Anyone who didn't fish was either too old to be out at sea, physically disabled, seriously injured or chronically tubercular. But maybe the reason the mute did not fish was simply because he was mute.

When the mute was not gesturing or using sign language, he appeared to be no different from anyone else, at least on the outside, but there was something hidden in his face, some profound malevolence and slyness. When he moved his hands in frenzied sign language, you could also see that he had an enormous black birthmark on the back of his hand. It seemed to me that the black birthmark possessed some sort of evil power over him.

I don't know why the mute chose me. Perhaps he knew that I was the village orphan, the only child in the village with neither a mother nor a father. Perhaps he knew that my grandparents hated each other and that there was no one else to take care of me. Perhaps he was simply aware that I was timid and helpless, unable to fight back or defend myself. Whatever the reason, at the age of seven I experienced my first terror of men. It was a terror that came in the form of the mute.

The mute lived on one of the lanes adjacent to Pirate's Alley. Pirate's Alley was the longest street in the village and was intersected at various points by a number of smaller alleyways. Like a giant fishing net, it gathered up the other alleyways and dragged them towards the coast and out to sea. It was so narrow and winding that, in some places, it was hard not to brush against the stone walls of the houses on either side, even when walking alone. The villagers, who often carried things on shoulder poles, had to estimate the angle of each turn well in advance if they wished safely to negotiate the twists and turns. The greenish cobblestones of the alley were always damp, drenched with saltwater spray from the ocean and freshwater spilled from buckets that the villagers carried down from the well on the far side of the mountain. The road was rough and uneven and the crevices between the cobblestones were filled with tiny shrimps and dead fish. It reminded me of the ocean floor, the Underwater lair of the Sea Demon.

As I threaded my way down the alley, past one narrow turn and then another, I never knew when or in which unexpected corner I might run into the mute. At first he didn't look dangerous. He would smile and gesture to me using his sign language, although I was never able to work out exactly what he was trying to say. But the moment there were no other people around, he would turn ugly and frightening, and begin to follow me. I would pretend to ignore him and continue on my way down the alley, but it soon became obvious from the sound of my footsteps that I was running, the mute close on my seven-year-old heels. I remember how he would follow me all the way to the end of Pirate's Alley, to the point at which the houses disappeared and the ocean came into view.

My favourite place in the Village of Stone was the old meeting

38

hall at the end of the peninsula. The hall had originally been used as headquarters by the local civilian militia, but now that they had nothing to do and no battles to fight, it was used for film screenings and performances by the local opera troupe. The films and operas shown there were well-known pieces such as *Dream of Red Mansions, The Emerald Hairpin, Gold Mountain Under Water* or *The Legend of Lady White Snake.* I loved to go and watch them, delighting in finding elaborate ways to sneak past the ticket collectors and avoid paying.

One afternoon, as I was walking idly down the alley, I saw the mute waiting for me. Instinctively I started to run towards the meeting hall, but when I reached it, I realised that a film had started. Where could I run? I ducked into the ladies' toilet. When I emerged a while later and dashed past the usher with his torch, I thought that I was safe, that I must have managed to lose the mute. I walked through the darkness and took a seat in the front row. The film was one I had seen many times before – *Meng Lijun* – but it was such a relief to feel safe that I soon found myself caught up in the familiar story of the young woman, Meng Lijun, who dresses up as a boy to rescue her father. A few minutes later, however, I saw the mute groping his way down the aisles. When he sat down next to me, I began to feel frightened, but I didn't dare to do anything. I was too frightened to scream, to run or, most of all, to cry. All I could do was watch as the mute stretched out his hand, pulled down the loose elastic waistband of my trousers and put his hand inside my clothes. His hand, with that hideous black birthmark, was like an enormous pair of tongs holding my body fast within its grip. He spent the entire film rubbing and pinching me through my underpants.

At seven, all I felt was a profound sense of shame. Shame was something that I had never felt before. It robbed me of any ability to scream, run away or defend myself. From the depths of my shame, I suffered that arm reaching into my underpants, that hand touching me, those fingers slowly moving over my flesh. The crime took place in darkness and in silence. The only

39

person talking, shouting, laughing, singing or screaming in the darkened hall was Meng Lijun, heroine of the silver screen.

After I had escaped from the hall, I ran down to the beach. I knew that if the fishermen's wives were still on the beach, the mute would not dare to come near me. He would affect a calm, collected air, as if he harboured not an evil thought in his mind, and stroll along the beach with both hands clasped behind his back.

From then on, the mute haunted every corner of my world. Every time I went to the fried cake stall, the spun sugar stand or the grain store, I would see the mute making his way towards me, a phantom made material. His hands seemed to hold some sort of absolute authority over my tiny, frail body. These were the hands that grabbed me, that pushed their fingers into me, that seemed to have as their sole goal in life the small space beneath my underpants. The mute seemed to have a supernatural sense of hearing, like the ghosts in old Chinese legends that could hear the slightest sound carried upon the wind. It was as if he were listening to my every step, as if he could hear through doors and walls of stone, down the entire length of Pirate's Alley.

One afternoon, I slipped into the courtyard compound belonging to the village operatic troupe. I loved this courtyard because, when it was not raining, the young male and female singers came out into it to practise their roles. Another thing I liked about the courtyard was its props storeroom, which held a multitude of treasures. I longed to be able to steal a set of white silk sleeves embroidered with flowers, a fake broadsword made of shiny tinfoil or, even better, the pearl-encrusted phoenix headdress that the lovely Xue Baocha wore at her wedding to the dashing Jia Baoyu in *Dream of Red Mansions*. Everything in that courtyard was lovely, even the people, particularly the beautiful young actresses who sang the ingénue roles. That day, however, the courtyard seemed to be deserted, and there was not a person in sight. I supposed that perhaps the troupe had gone to another province to put on a performance. If so, the timing was perfect, for it meant that I could slip unseen into the storeroom and steal the phoenix headdress that I so coveted. But when I entered the storeroom, I found it empty. The rows of white silk sleeves that usually hung along the wall were gone, along with all the fake swords, red tassels and other props. I stared for a moment in surprise, and then began wandering about the dimly lit storeroom. The sunlight pouring through the cracks in the roof illuminated motes of dust floating through the air. Suddenly the storeroom felt stifling, and the clouds of dust were making it hard for me to breathe. As I turned to leave, I saw a shadow emerge from the darkness. It was the mute.

There he stood, towering over me like the heavenly generals who descend from the skies in Chinese opera. He just stood there, grinning at me. I was so frightened that I began to tremble, for I knew that there was no one in the courtyard to help me. So I ran. I raced into the deserted cafeteria, the mute close on my heels. When I turned around to look behind me, I could see that he was swiftly gaining ground. His face was contorted and terrifying, like a hideous mask. Desperate now, I ran out of the cafeteria and bolted upstairs to the first floor, where I knew that some of the bit players occasionally slept. But as I rounded the first-floor landing, the mute, quicker and more nimble, caught up and grabbed me around the waist. Like a dog with an especially keen sense of hearing, he paused for a moment to listen and then, apparently satisfied that he had heard nothing, seemed to fly into a rage. This time, he did not content himself with touching me through my underpants. Instead, he abruptly yanked my trousers down, so that my lower body was completely exposed to his gaze. I was terror-stricken. In his clutches I was like a lamb to the slaughter, yet I didn't dare scream. I was certain that if I did, he would kill me.

At that moment, I heard footsteps on the staircase, as if someone were coming downstairs. The mute must have heard them, too, for he quickly pulled my trousers back up, wheeled around and made his escape down the stairs. Standing alone on the landing where the mute had left me, I caught sight of two

grown-ups descending the staircase, and the flicker of a cigarette lighter. The men glanced briefly at my tearstained face as
they passed, but took no further notice of me. I trailed down
the staircase after them and, staying close on their heels, followed
them out of the courtyard and all the way to the bus station
on the outskirts of the village. As I watched the two men walk
into the station ticket office, I finally mustered the courage to
turn my head and look behind me. The mute was nowhere to
be seen.

I was afraid to leave the station right away because I thought
that the mute might be waiting for me somewhere nearby. I
paced around for a while, watching a tractor that had come to
the village to pick up a shipment of fish. The tractor driver was
obviously not from the Village of Stone. His face was not the
face of a sea scavenger, and his skin was neither tanned brown
from the sun nor chapped red by the wind. He was supervising
two fishermen who were loading large wicker baskets into the
passenger seat of his tractor. The baskets were filled with fish
and squid. When the tractor was loaded full, the driver would
drive back to where he had come from, but where that might
be, I had no idea.

The station was a very safe place because the stationmaster,
whom everyone called 'Old Crippled Son of the Sea', was the
nicest person in the village. I wasn't sure why, but every time
Old Crippled Son of the Sea saw the mute hanging around the
station, he would scold him or issue a pointed reminder that
he was keeping an eye on him. For this reason, the village mute
never dared to go to the bus station.

As I approached the ticket office, I could see Old Crippled
Son of the Sea sitting at his desk, illuminated by the bare bulb
overhead. His bifocals were perched on the bridge of his nose
and he was busily stamping a long, narrow book of bus tickets
with an official seal. I longed to have my own stamped and
validated bus ticket so that I could get on a bus and ride away
from the Village of Stone. I didn't even care where the bus
went, as long as it left the village.

I leaned against the window of the ticket office and watched Old Crippled Son of the Sea at his work. I hoped that he would come outside and help me, but he seemed so terribly busy, bustling first to one task and then another. I don't know how he got such a strange name. As long as I could remember, everyone in the village had called him Old Crippled Son of the Sea. Probably his parents gave him the name 'Son of the Sea', and then the villagers added the 'Crippled' after he injured his leg and the 'Old' with increasing age. Despite this rather odd name, he was a very powerful man in the Village of Stone. Since he was the only person working at the bus station, he was stationmaster, ticket seller, ticket puncher and, occasionally, even bus driver, all wrapped into one. Of all of the non-sea scavengers in the Village of Stone, he was the busiest. He was also the most selfless person in the village. I had heard people say that the stationmaster was a member of the Communist Party. At the time, I didn't know what it meant to be a member of the Communist Party, but I gathered that it was no easy achievement. If a man as great as my neighbour the Sea Captain, Boy Waiting's father, was not a member of the Communist Party, then Old Crippled Son of the Sea must be a very great man indeed.

I once saw the stationmaster sell a whole busload of tickets. The passengers – young and old, male and female, some carrying fish or shouldering heavy coils of rope – were all standing waiting for a seat on a vomit-splattered long-distance bus. Even the stationmaster's wife, a woman with a pockmarked face who worked in the seaweed beds along the shore, was at the station that day. She must have been planning to travel on the bus, for I noticed that she carried a bag with her and was waiting by the door of the bus. I guessed that she was allowed to get on first because she was the stationmaster's wife. At last, the station-master, carrying a set of keys, approached the bus. When he saw that the passengers were not queued up properly he began to bellow, 'Line up! Line up!' Then he picked up the whistle hanging around his neck and gave a sharp blow. At the sound of the whistle, everyone immediately queued up in a straight line. When everyone was lined up with military precision, the stationmaster inspected the queue from head to tail. Seeming to notice a problem, he rushed forward, grabbed his pockmarked wife by the shirtsleeve and transferred her from her position at the head of the queue to the very end. Even as he did this, he continued shouting for the passengers to line up. Judging from the expression on his wife's face, she was extremely displeased at being forced to the back, but the stationmaster had the satisfied look of a good Communist who had followed Mao's precept not to favour one's family.

Because Old Crippled Son of the Sea was in charge of selling tickets, anyone who wanted to buy a bus ticket had to answer all his questions about where they were going, and why, and how long they would be staying. All the villagers dutifully answered the stationmaster's questions. He was very helpful as well, always quick to offer passengers advice about their planned destinations, things to be wary of and a variety of other useful information.

I longed to ask the old stationmaster if I could buy a ticket, but, if I did, he would be certain to ask me where I wanted to go, and the only place I knew was the Village of Stone. And how could he possibly sell me a bus ticket? He would probably tell my grandparents, and I knew that my grandmother would never let me leave the village. Anyway, how could I think of leaving the Village of Stone? If I left, I was sure that I could never survive on my own.

If only I had been able to tell the stationmaster about the mute. Yet for many years, an overwhelming shame and terror conspired to keep me silent. I was so enveloped by the enormity of my shame that I lost the courage to seek out the protection of other people. I didn't dare speak to my grandmother because I knew that she herself was a person who had been consumed by shame her entire life. Our home at Number 13 Pirate's Alley was a house of shame. Meanwhile Number 14, Boy Waiting's house, was always filled with the sound of seven daughters laughing, squabbling, skipping or shelling shrimp. I envied them their days together. In our house, every day was spent in silence. My grandparents rarely spoke to me, nor did I speak to them. We were like a family of mutes who still retained the power of speech. I had no real friends and nobody to talk to. Everyone thought I was an odd child, even Boy Waiting, who had failed to bring her parents a baby brother, and Number Three, a little girl with an ugly swollen right cheek. Though I was as coarse and unruly as my childhood playmates, they never really considered me one of their gang.

From the age of seven, I lived with the bleak expectation that the mute would be with me until the day I died. Or until the day he died. There was only one way to extricate myself from this shame and terror. One of us would have to die.

I began to wish for death: either my death, or the mute's. No matter which one of us died, it would be a good thing.

7

Death, when it did arrive, struck where it was least expected.

The night Death cast its shadow on our house there were no typhoon winds or fierce rains; even the fishing boats had come home safely. Through the stone walls, I could hear the sound of their outboard motors chugging along the shore.

My grandmother was already asleep when my grandfather descended the stairs. I was lying next to her beneath a home-made indigo-dyed quilt, my head resting on a pillow filled with husked rice that crackled each time I moved. I could hear my grandfather coming down the stairs as he usually did, making the turn at the first-floor landing without bothering to stop. When he reached the ground floor, he paused for a moment, as if he were looking for something. Then he opened the wooden front door, which creaked loudly on its hinges, and slipped outside, shutting the door quietly on his way out. I imagined that he was going out to buy liquor or some peanuts, as he often did when he could not sleep. He would go out for a drink or two, after which he would return home to bed. I thought I had guessed correctly, for I soon heard him come in again and close the door behind him. As he slowly climbed the stairs to the second floor, I could hear the clink of a bottle in his hand. My grandmother, lying on the cold bamboo bed, turned over softly in her sleep and sighed.

My grandmother was always sighing. I think her sighs were an expression of her dissatisfaction with life and her inability to fight back, as if she were trying to grab hold of something with both hands tied behind her back. Every day of my grandmother's life was a sigh. When my grandfather was younger, he often beat and cursed her violently, and treated her no better than he would a servant. When my grandparents grew older the beatings stopped, but the cursing and beating had been their only real form of interaction. When that ceased, my grandparents became strangers to each other. Even hatred has to age, I suppose. My grandparents had certainly aged. They had lost all their teeth, their backs had grown bent and now all they had left were their sighs. That evening, to the accompaniment of my grandmother's mournful sighing, my grandfather climbed upstairs and went to bed, never to rise again.

My grandfather committed suicide. He purchased a bottle of DDV, an extremely poisonous agricultural pesticide, and chased it down with a bottle of sorghum whisky and some salted peanuts.

We did not discover his body until the middle of the following day.

My grandmother did not seem particularly concerned when my grandfather did not rise from bed as usual that morning. She behaved just as she did every other morning. She trimmed the wicks, lit the stove, boiled some water in a pan and proceeded to heat up the scant remains of the previous day's gruel. To the gruel she added a piece of brownish toffee we called Tangjiu toffee. The toffee was made from dough containing wheat flour and brown sugar, which was kneaded until it became firm and elastic. Afterwards the dough was pressed into a patterned wooden mould, cooked, and dried until it solidified. Tangjiu toffee was so hard that it took a very long time to soften in a bowl of gruel. I imagined that my grandfather would be out of bed by the time the toffee had softened. But there had still been no sign of movement from above when my grandmother lifted the lid of the pot to look inside and saw that the toffee had already softened so much that the pattern on its surface, two magpies perched on the branch of a tree, was blurred. She cocked her head towards the ceiling. She seemed mystified that my grandfather had done none of the things he normally did each morning. We had not heard him cough or seen him carrying his chamber pot downstairs to empty it. Still more strange, he had not gone to draw water from the well on the other side of the mountain. Perhaps he was sick. Still, my grandmother said nothing. She gave me some of the toffee and made herself a bowl of gruel with lobster paste. I sat on the threshold, gazing blankly across the street at the small hairdresser's shop opposite and wondering whether the mute would appear that day. I nibbled at my toffee, taking one small bite after another, and listened as my grandmother finished her gruel and began reciting her second sutra of the day. Above the hearth, there was a white porcelain figure of Guanyin, the Goddess of Mercy, to whom my grandmother addressed her daily prayers. My grandmother always prayed to Guanyin rather than to Mazu Niangniang, perhaps because she felt the Sea Goddess was too partial to the sea scavengers. Ten minutes later, my grandmother had finished reciting her second sutra and I had finished eating my toffee, and my grandfather still had not come downstairs. I left the house and made my way down the street and onto the beach, as I did every day. I was still too young to go to school and I would play on the beach all day long, until the sun had disappeared behind the hills and I could hear my grandmother's old, mournful cries echoing down the beach: 'Little Dog! Little Dog, get yourself home to eat!'

When I reached the beach, I found that none of the fishermen had gone out to sea that day. Instead, the beach was filled with the clamour of voices and crowds of fishermen who were repairing their boats. The overturned boats, their white bellies facing skyward, looked like upended turtles sprawled on the sand. Some of the fishermen had set up ladders so that they could crawl onto their boats to make repairs. Others carried cans of brightly coloured paint or were already busy covering the hulls of their boats with layer after layer of paint. I remembered that my grandfather had once told me that it was terribly important to paint the boats properly. You had to make sure that there were enough layers of paint, because the greater the number of layers, the greater a boat's ability to ply through the waves. You also had to be careful about the way you painted the eyes. The eyes should be two colours, red and black. If the eyes were not well painted, the Sea Demon would be sure to capsize the boat. A boat with eyes could see its way through the typhoon waves and better scavenge the sea.

I spent that morning, the morning before anyone in the village had any inkling of my grandfather's suicide, standing idly in the sunshine and salt air, watching the fishermen. I did not suspect that this day would turn out to be different from any other. Whether the fishermen set out to sea or stayed in for repairs or painted eyes on their boats made no difference to my grandfather. He hadn't been to sea for decades. These activities held no meaning or omens for him.

I began to feel hungry. My belly had already digested the toffee I had eaten earlier that morning. The mute had not appeared, so I thought it was safe to go home and eat lunch. I didn't care whether I ate my grandmother's lunch of mushy gruel with shrimp paste or my grandfather's lunch of pork. Either was fine with me.

When I returned home at noon, the house was completely silent. I touched the stove and found it cold. I knew that my grandmother had just returned from drawing water from the well on the other side of the mountain, because I could see puddles where the water had spilled from the buckets and onto the black stone floor. My grandmother looked exhausted. Her back was bent and her hair dishevelled, falling around her cheeks in snowy wisps. Her wrinkles, piled one upon another like the steps in the Village of Stone, were tanned dark from the sun. As she sat near the threshold, wiping the sweat from her face and sighing to herself, I realised how old she looked, how terribly old! She had aged so much that she hardly seemed human. Looking at my grandmother, I suddenly became afraid. I felt as if I were going to cry, for I was terrified that one day I would be as old as she was. My grandfather had not gone to the well that morning, so my grandmother had taken it upon herself to draw water from the well. I watched as she took up a ladle and began to scoop water from the buckets and pour it into the vat where we stored our fresh water. The vat was so large and so deep that I feared I would drown if I ever fell into it.

After my grandmother had emptied one bucket of water, she sat down again, wiped the sweat from her brow and heaved a long sigh. Nervously, I walked over to the stove, stood on a stool and peeked inside the pot my grandmother used for making toffee. The toffee had congealed, and was now the consistency of a slab of metal. I was disappointed because I knew that my grandmother, after going to the well to draw water, would be too exhausted to make another meal that day. I wanted to go up to the second floor and eat lunch with my grandfather, but he had not called me yet, nor had I heard the sounds of cooking. Unsure what to do, I grabbed a handful of dried, salted shrimp from the kitchen cupboard and washed them down with a few glasses of cold water. By now, my grandmother was growing restless, pacing back and forth around the kitchen, idly touching this and that. She appeared to be preoccupied, but still she made no move to do anything. Was she worried that my grandfather was so late getting out of bed? I didn't know. All I knew was that I had a belly full of cold water and that the dried shrimp I had just eaten were beginning to churn in my stomach. At that moment my grandmother, unable to stand it any longer, walked towards me and pointed upstairs. I understood immediately that she wanted me to go up to the second floor and see what my grandfather was doing.

I climbed the stairs. When I reached the first-floor landing, the house was silent. The only sound was the wind rattling the windows and doors of the house. I assumed that my grandfather had drunk too much the night before and was still in bed, sleeping. At the second-floor landing I noticed a terrible smell, rather like alcohol but more chemical. I held my nose and entered the room, but when I reached my grandfather's bed-side, I froze in shock.

My grandfather's mouth was covered with white foam. His features were contorted in pain, his face a shade of bluish-purple that I had never seen before. The only thing I recognised was his familiar mane of white hair.

I stepped forward and tried to shake my grandfather awake. I thought he must be sleeping, for I had no idea what death looked like. First I tugged at his arm. When he did not react, I used both hands to shake him with much greater force, but he remained inert. I began to call out to him, my shouts growing louder and louder. Still there was no reaction.

My grandmother, as usual, did not even come upstairs.

Terror-stricken, I raced downstairs and told my grandmother, 'Grandpa's sleeping, and I can't wake him up!'

My grandmother reacted as if she had been struck by light-ning. Her eyes filled with tears and she began to weep. When I realised that my grandmother was actually crying, I began to feel truly afraid. She rushed towards the staircase and began to climb the stairs. Trailing after her as she laboured up, one slow step after another, I realised for the first time how very steep our staircase was. I wondered how many years it had been since my grandmother had last been to the second floor. How many years had passed since the last time she had entered my grand-father's room? Ten years? Twenty, even thirty years?

'He's dead. He drank poison.' These were my grandmother's words as she stood by my grandfather's bed. She began to cry once more, her tears falling onto the bottle of poison on the floor.

Was this how people died? I stood barefoot, beside the empty bottle of poison, feeling terribly confused.

I knew nothing about death, in the same way that I knew nothing about birth. Was death the same thing as sleep? If you fell asleep and never woke up, did that mean you were dead?

Though I had often anticipated my own death or the death

of the mute, I now realised that it was not something to be taken lightly. Death was a terrifying thing.

When four men from the coffin maker's shop entered the house carrying my grandfather's red lacquer casket and my grand-mother came out of the kitchen to meet them, she appeared extremely disoriented. Outside our house stood an electricity pole that provided us with a few hours of rationed electricity a day. It had been charred black in a fire. My grandmother stepped over the high threshold and, walking over to the pole, wrapped her arms tightly around it, then suddenly slumped to the ground and began wailing. She sounded like a madwoman, her loud wailing punctuated now and then by an unintelligible mumbling. A crowd of people began to gather around our door. At first it was only children, then fishermen's wives, then old women on their way home from the fish market, still clutching their nets full of squirming shrimp. In the end, even the village fishermen joined the crowd. I thought I caught a glimpse of the mute and my heart skipped a beat, but when I looked again, he seemed to have disappeared into the crowd. If he knew what had happened, I hoped, maybe he wouldn't ever bother me again . . . I dashed into the house, hid myself in one of the darkened corners of the kitchen and refused to come out again. It was too bright outside, but the kitchen was nice and dark. Nobody would be able to see me.

As the babble of voices outside grew louder, I overheard several of the fishermen's wives gossiping.

'The old girl never got along with her old man while he was alive. Now that he's dead, what on earth is she crying about?'

'You don't understand. She has to cry. If she doesn't cry, it means she isn't loyal.'

A third woman broke in, 'That's right. Even if she doesn't feel like crying, she has to fake it, at least. Because if she doesn't cry in this life, she'll be crying in the next one!'

I listened to my grandmother crying for a very long time.

Her sobbing seemed endless. It was pitiful, yet not a single person in the crowd had any sympathy for her. She cried until her tears dried up, as if she had cried out all the moisture in her body. Clad in mourning black, racked with sobs and clinging to that blackened electricity pole, her body seemed frailer somehow, more shrunken.

My grandmother exhausted our ears with her sobbing. As for me, I never shed a tear.

That whole day, I hid in the shadows of the house and refused to come out because I did not want anyone in the street to see me. All the spectators gathered outside our door were adults and children I knew from the village. Even the old station-master, the most upstanding resident of the Village of Stone, was there, along with his pockmarked wife. It was as if an entire theatre performance had moved from the village auditorium to Number 13, Pirate's Alley. Only this time, we weren't performing *Five Filial Daughters Wish Their Mother Longevity*. We were putting on a tragedy, and everyone knows how much people love a good tragedy. I was completely humiliated. I felt as if there were no way I could go on living in the Village of Stone, not after this.

Inside the house, the coffin makers were busy putting the finishing touches to the casket. My grandmother was still outside, crying. I ran upstairs, hoping to escape the noise of the crowd and my grandmother's infuriating wailing. When I reached the second floor, I saw my grandfather's new funeral clothes laid out neatly on my grandmother's bamboo bed. It had taken a local seamstress a whole day and night to finish sewing the black silk clothes in time for the funeral. My grandfather had never worn such fine clothes during his lifetime. I touched the silk and thought: *These are things for the dead*. I don't know why, but it frightened me. As I stared blankly at the brand new funeral clothes, the sound of voices from the street reached my ears.

'You know why the old man did it, don't you? Because he wasn't happy.'

'Of course he wasn't happy. He had no boat, his son was unfilial and, as if that weren't enough, his wife was bad luck!'

'His whole life was a tragedy. He had no children to look after him in his old age. Why else would he kill himself? He must have done something wrong in a previous life to be cursed with such bad luck . . .'

'You could say the same about his wife. That's probably why they ended up together . . .'

I leaned out of the window and looked down. The coffin makers had left, my grandmother had cried herself to exhaustion and the crowd outside was starting to disperse. Even the fishermen's wives who had taken such pleasure in the spectacle began to leave, chattering among themselves as they returned home to finish their housework. The only ones left were the children, always indefatigable. So many children had gathered at our front door that they naturally fell to playing together. I saw Boy Waiting and two or three of her older sisters among them. The children were busy playing storm the fortress, swapping cigarette cards and getting into fights. The boys threw kicks and punches; the girls pulled each other's plaits.

Eventually, my grandmother stopped crying and returned to her usual silence. It seemed as if she had cried enough to last a lifetime. She simply stopped in mid-sob, pulled herself up from the foot of the charred electricity pole and walked back into the house. After all, the coffin had arrived and there was work to be done preparing the body for the funeral.

My grandmother first set to bathing my grandfather's body. While she washed his hands, his back and the soles of his feet, I helped by drawing fresh water. When she had finished bathing him, she began to dress him in his burial clothes. As she lifted his shoulders, I was shocked to see how rigid my grandfather's body had become. His limbs were as inflexible as metal bars, and his joints popped loudly when my grandmother tried to lift his arms. It was impossible to get my grandfather's arms into the sleeves of his funeral clothes. His hands were a terrible shade of bluish-purple, the fingers curled like talons, the veins

54

bulging visibly beneath his skin. I had never seen my grand-father's hands look like that, more like claws than human hands. I stood frozen at my grandmother's side, staring at those awful hands. Could these be the same hands that had once spread green fishing nets, studded with colourful floats, on the surface of the ocean? The same hands that had pulled in nets full of shrimp and squirming fish somewhere on the open sea, far from shore? The hands that had once brandished fists at my silent grandmother in this three-storey house of stone? And though they now looked like the claws of a crab, these must be the same hands that had opened a bottle of poison and held it up to his mouth.

Once again, I heard my grandfather's joints pop. The sound gave me gooseflesh. I glanced at my grandmother and saw that she had only been able to get my grandfather's arms halfway into his sleeves, and yet her forehead was already covered with beads of sweat from the exertion. She sat down dejectedly on the bed, beside her dead husband, and wiped the sweat from her brow. Her voice listless, my grandmother ordered me to go next door and fetch Boy Waiting's mother.

I rushed next door. Boy Waiting was not at home, but I found her mother sitting in the courtyard shelling shrimp. She was heavily pregnant. The cobblestone courtyard was covered with mountains of slippery white shrimp and their discarded heads and shells. I knew that when Boy Waiting's mother had finished drying and salting the shrimp, she would sell them to the seafood cold processing plant, where they fetched seven cents per pound. I knew this because I had helped Boy Waiting shell shrimp many times. Boy Waiting's mother spent most of her spare time shelling shrimp, and the tips of her fingers were bleached white from the salt water.

Breathlessly, I ran towards her and blurted, 'She can't . . . the clothes . . . she can't put the clothes on!'

Boy Waiting's mother stopped what she was doing and asked, 'The clothes?'

'She can't put them on. The arms . . . they're too stiff!' I let my head drop sideways and raised my arms in a pantomime of a dead person.

Boy Waiting's mother understood immediately. She brushed off her apron and heaved her pregnant body up from the bench, scattering shrimp left and right. Without another word, she hurried out of the courtyard and towards our house. Boy Waiting's mother was a truly kind woman.

I was reluctant to go home, so I wandered around the court-yard a bit. Boy Waiting's family had a fragrant jasmine tree in full bloom in the middle of their courtyard. It was wonderful. There was a long shallow basket, perched on two benches, filled with cuttlefish drying in the sun. Beneath the jasmine tree, there were also several yellow fishing floats and a pile of green nylon used for weaving fishing nets.

My grandmother often told me that everyone had past, present and future lives. If I had a future life, I hoped I could be re-incarnated into Boy Waiting's family, so that I could finally be one of them. Boy Waiting had many older sisters, so I would never need to worry about having no one to talk to. Even at night, I would never be lonely. So many times I had dreamed that Boy Waiting's mother was my own mother, and the Captain my very own father. In my dreams, I was just like Boy Waiting, surrounded by older sisters, all those little girls that Boy Waiting's mother had given birth to. We ran around, laughing and teasing and pulling each other's plaits. In my dreams, I wasn't afraid of death, because our house was so full of people, so full of life. Everywhere was the sound of joyful laughter. I wasn't afraid of the mute either, because my father was a big strong fishing boat captain. He was brave and tall and nobody could beat him in a fight, not even the mute. I felt safe and happy in those recur-ring dreams, but when I awoke I discovered that I was still lying on my grandmother's bamboo bed. The bed was always cold. My white-haired grandmother lay beside me breathing feebly, and the ocean breezes that preceded a typhoon whistled monot-onously through the wooden shutters. In the silence between each gust of wind and the next, I could hear my grandfather snoring upstairs or, on nights when he could not sleep, tossing and turning on his bed made of palm wood. Night after night I would hear the whoosh, whoosh, whoosh of those indefatigable waves beating on the reef. And night after night, there was no jasmine tree, no pile of fishing floats, no coil of green nylon rope and no basket filled with cuttlefish drying in the sun. There was no laughter from Boy Waiting's older sisters and there was no father with his own fishing boat – my dream father, my father in a future life. I was still Little Dog, a seven-year-old girl nobody cared about, a strange child nobody wanted, not even the Sea Demon.

In the endless midnight that loomed before me after waking, I began to see that my dreams were nothing more than idle fantasy. Although that dream was taking place right on the other side of my wall, just next door in that jasmine-scented court-yard, I would never be able to scale that wall because it didn't belong to me. This was my life, the only life that the gods in charge of this world had seen fit to grant me.

My grandfather's funeral was held on the far side of the mountain. It was a place covered with weeds and headstones marking the graves where generation after generation of fishermen and their wives had been buried. As you rounded the top of the hill, you could glimpse two headstones, side by side. The grass around the headstones was not very high, thanks to my grandmother's careful tending. These were the graves that my grandparents had chosen as their final resting place many years earlier, when my grandmother was still very young and had just entered my grandfather's household. Though she was now an old woman devoid of language, devoid of happiness, you had to admit that she had chosen a lovely gravesite for herself: the vast blue sea at the foot of the mountain stretched as far as eyes could see, seagulls flew overhead, coasting on rays of sunlight, and the valley below was filled with row upon row of closely planted pines. Each evening at dusk, the gravesite afforded a view of the deep red setting sun as it made its plunge into the sea.

When my grandfather's coffin had been lowered into the ground, my grandmother made me kneel before the grave and touch my head to the earth three times. As I kowtowed, my grandmother began burning offerings of paper coins. She had been up all night making the coins, tearing sheets of cheap brown paper into tiny pieces. In his lifetime, my grandfather never seemed to have enough money. Some of the villagers even called him a miser, citing his unwillingness to spend any money at all on my grandmother. In the afterworld, among all those dead souls and demons, my grandfather would not need to worry about money, for I knew that, as long as she lived, my grandmother would burn a large number of paper coins for him each and every year. After my grandfather's death, my grandmother finally had the chance to be a good wife.

I finished kowtowing in a daze, then stood up and brushed the mountain dirt from my knees. While the black-clad monks surrounded the grave and began beating their wooden fish in time to the chanting of the sutras, I quietly slipped away. I could not bear to linger any longer. I stood back and watched from afar as my grandmother drew a handful of paper notes from a large wicker basket and tossed them into the fire. After my grandfather's grave had been covered with earth, I gazed at the empty grave beside it, my grandmother's grave. I wondered if she were eager to be put into that silent ground as soon as possible, eager to be surrounded by the sound of the ocean and the wind through the pines. After all, was there any reason to want to linger in this life?

No one was able to locate my absentee father to give him the news of my grandfather's death or to tell him the truth about what had happened. Although who really knew the truth? Nobody knew why my grandfather had killed himself or why he had decided to drink poison. Though my grandfather could write, he had not left a suicide note. He had written down no complaints or reasons for his suicide; he had given us no hints. Likewise, he had given me no hints about either my past or my future. One night, as he listened to the sound of the ocean tide coming in through a small second-floor window, he had simply decided that he wanted to die. He had left nothing to my grandmother, for he had nothing to give. Not a sampan, not a skiff, not even a torn fishing net.

In among all the memories bound up in that silent house of stone, I try to recall the things that my grandfather said to me while he was alive. He was always so cold and distant. My grandmother feared him, as did I. To us, he was just the view of a back moving upstairs or downstairs, a back that never bothered to turn towards us, a back that radiated no visible warmth and communicated no information at all. There is one conversation in the mists of my memory, however, that is different from the rest.

One day, my grandfather came down the stairs as I was standing at the window, watching the rain inundate the street outside. For no particular reason, he called my name. 'Little Dog . . .'

I made a little grunt by way of reply, wondering why he had decided to speak to me.

These are the words my grandfather spoke: 'If you ever meet your father, Little Dog, tell him that I was an unhappy man.'

'My father?' I was confused. 'But I thought you said he was never coming back.'

At first my grandfather did not reply. After a moment, he said, 'Oh, that's right. I forgot.'

With this, he turned away, picked up an umbrella from behind the door and walked out into the rain.

I think that was the only time that my grandfather ever said anything to me about his attitude towards life. I suppose it was his way of telling my father, the father I had never met, about his own unhappiness.

I had absolutely no concept of the word father. As far as I was concerned, he was a man who didn't exist.

My memory grows foggy. No matter how hard I try to recall my grandfather's face, I can't quite remember what he looked like. I begin to regret that I never touched his face with my own hands, not even once. I think that if a person never touches the face of another with his or her very own hand, then that person will eventually forget what the other looked like.

And so when I think of my grandfather, I think of him picking up that umbrella and walking out into the rain-drenched street. I think of his back disappearing down Pirate's Alley, that back that never radiated any warmth, and never even bothered to turn round.

8

The day I received the parcel of eel began badly. Red stumbled groggily into the bathroom to use the toilet. Only too late did he realise that the toilet would not flush because the pipes were clogged. Using a plunger and a variety of other household implements, Red tried to get the toilet to flush, but in vain: the water refused to swirl down into the porcelain vortex. Water spilled over the edge of the toilet bowl and onto the floor, transforming the bathroom into a swamp. Red bailed as fast as he could, but the unbearable stench spread through our entire flat. At this point, we began to consider ourselves fortunate to live on the ground floor. At least we did not have to worry about our toilet water flooding any neighbours below. Living on the ground floor of a high-rise building, it seems, is not entirely without its advantages. As for the pipes becoming clogged, Red insisted that this was not our fault. He admitted to having tossed cigarette butts into the toilet on occasion, but even a hundred cigarette butts, he reasoned, would not be enough to clog the pipes. I also admitted to having thrown things into the toilet, such as the tiny balls of hair that accumulated during our daily showers, but I doubted they would have caused a blockage in the pipes. In the end, Red and I concurred that blocked pipes were the collective fault of those thousands of other residents above us; we simply had the misfortune to share their plumbing. They were the ones up there every day eating, drinking, shitting and pissing to their hearts' content. We were just the innocent victims on the ground floor.

Red, naked from the waist down, picked up a mop and

angrily waded into the lake that had once been our bathroom. He began to mop up as best he could, but this went no way towards solving the fundamental problem. The toilet was still clogged. He threw on an overcoat and went out to find the person in charge of building plumbing maintenance. I could not bear to stay inside our flat a moment longer, so I brushed my teeth in the kitchen and headed over to a nearby supermarket to buy some milk.

As I passed the mailboxes in the hallway, I checked to see if we had any mail. I was surprised to find a notice stating that there was a package waiting for me at the post office. My name and address were written clearly in the box marked 'recipient'. Under 'place of origin', someone had written 'Village of Stone'. I stood rooted to the spot staring at the name of the place I had tried to avoid thinking about for over ten years. A shiver of anxiety ran through me at the idea that someone from the village was trying to contact me. I held the notice up to the sunlight and tried to make out the sender's name, but it was rendered completely illegible by a large ink-blot. I gave up and began instead to puzzle over what might be in the package. In the space marked 'Contents', someone had written 'edibles'. I glanced at the notice one last time and tucked it carefully into my pocket.

At the store, I bought a large carton of San Yuan brand milk and hurried home. When I opened the burglar-proof metal door to our flat, I discovered that Red had already tidied up the bathroom and managed to resolve the toilet problem. He was standing inside the bathroom, spraying air freshener. When he had finished, he picked up a large bag of refuse and walked over to the doorway where I was standing.

'This place is a living hell,' he said as he went out and tossed the bag into the rubbish chute in the hallway.

'Just watch. Tomorrow it will be the rubbish chute that packs up.' He was still complaining as he walked back into the kitchen to wash his hands. 'Next thing you know, it will be the gas . . .'

I struck a match and put the kettle on, just to give myself

something to do. I had no desire to make coffee or tea, or anything else for that matter. I was still mulling over the notice in my pocket.

I kicked off my slippers, changed into a pair of sandals and informed Red that I was going to the post office.

'Why?' he asked. 'Are you going to send a letter?'

'Have you ever known me to send a letter?'

'Well, if you're going there to subscribe to a newspaper, sign me up for a six-month subscription to *Sports World News* while you're at it.'

'I'm not going there to get a subscription.'

'Why else would you go to the post office? It's not likely anyone sent you a money transfer.'

'Has it ever occurred to you that someone might have sent me a package?'

'Really?'

'Yeah.'

'It's probably some video company sending you movies for the shop.'

'I doubt it. All our videos are pirated.'

'What else could it be, then?'

'I have no idea.' I pocketed my identification card and started for the door.

Having failed to elicit any useful information from me, Red seemed to lose interest in the topic. As I closed the door, I could hear him spraying the flat with another round of air freshener.

The whole way to the post office, I tried to think who could possibly have sent me a package. I went through a mental list of the people I knew in the Village of Stone, but I had lost touch with all of them long ago. I had moved house so many times over the years that I could not imagine how anyone from the Village of Stone could possibly know my current address.

When I reached the post office, I lined up at the package delivery window and waited for about five minutes while the clerk rummaged through the disorderly storeroom. He finally emerged with a large white cloth parcel, which he tossed onto the counter with a thump.

I picked up the mysterious parcel and examined it carefully. First I held it to my nose and sniffed. The overpowering odour of salted fish assaulted my nostrils. It was a familiar smell, one that I remembered well. Images of all the different types of seafood in the Village of Stone flashed before my eyes. Perhaps it was one of the local fish, such as cuttlefish, butterfish, yellow croaker or hairtail. Or maybe it was oysters, prawns, Buddha Hand scallops, mussels or some other shellfish that lived in the tide pools of the Village of Stone. I examined the opening of the parcel and noticed that it had been sewn shut, although the seam had already burst in several places. Judging from the crudeness of the stitches, I guessed them to be a man's handiwork. There were two seams, as if the man had been worried that the package might come open and so had decided to add another line of stitching.

I gazed at the two rows of stitches and tried to imagine someone familiar, some man I knew, standing at the counter of the village post office as he stitched the package. There was only one post office in the Village of Stone. I remembered the old man in glasses who always sat near the door, ready to help illiterate villagers write their letters. He did good business and his calligraphy was competent, though rather slow, as he traced out each ideograph as painstakingly as if he were making a painting. His pace was well suited to the illiterate villagers, who were generally slow to put their thoughts into words. In the post office there was also a long table with a pot of water-diluted paste, and next to that, a tangled ball of rough cotton thread and a few large needles used for sewing packages. The needles, which always seemed to be bent, were thrust into an old chunk of crumbling sea sponge. It was as if long years of use, or the accumulated pressure of so many pairs of hands, had somehow bent the needles out of shape. Were the villagers still using the same old set of bent sewing needles all these years later? Were the needles covered in rust by now, I wondered, or had they been replaced by new ones?

I borrowed a pair of scissors from the stamp counter and cut into the package.

Inside was a black plastic bag, and inside the bag lay the monstrous dried eel.

Who could have sent this to me? And how on earth did they find me?

As I stared down at the eel, I suddenly began to feel frightened. It was as if I were trapped within the unseeing gaze of those dead eyes, caught in the power of the Eel Demon and unable to move.

At the package counter, there was a constant stream of people coming and going, carrying parcels to be posted or lugging parcels that they had received. But as soon as they caught sight of me holding the enormous eel, every one of them stopped to stare. One man even made a point of coming over to tap the eel on the head with his finger, as if to confirm that it was not, in fact, constructed of wood. Filled with misgivings, I carefully replaced the smelly creature in its parcel and lifted it gingerly, as one might a newborn infant.

I must have given Red quite a shock when I returned home and tossed an enormous salted eel onto the table.

At first, Red was not even sure what it was. Why anyone would want to salt and dry such an enormous piece of seafood was completely beyond his imagination. After asking where it came from, he just stood and stared, until at last he could no longer stand the fishy odour. Grumbling that he couldn't believe he was having to deal with yet another bad smell in the course of one day, he raced around the flat flinging windows open one by one. When this proved insufficient to drive out the stench, Red threw open the front door. Our flat was now open to the public.

Before long, the draught in the flat had intensified to a cross-current. Air raced from the open windows to the open door and back again, setting everything flapping in the breeze. The flat was like a boat being tossed by waves on an open sea, and anything that was not anchored down was in danger of being swept away. Only the enormous dried eel on the kitchen table remained unmoved. I heard the hesitant footsteps of someone outside in the hallway. A curious neighbour, most likely, but I was too embarrassed to go and see. The person outside must have been equally embarrassed, for the footsteps soon halted, then moved off into the distance. But a few minutes later, I heard the click of heels in the hall once again. Like a fly attracted by the smell of rotting meat, the persistent neighbour had returned.

There was jazz playing on the stereo, Billie Holiday's languid rendition of *I'm a Fool to Want You.* I had the strange sensation that the spirit of the dried eel was being channelled through Billie Holiday's voice, poking gentle fun at itself by way of her lyrics, and that everything in the house – the walls, the furnishings, even the curtains swaying in the breeze – was oddly complicit in this bizarre scene.

'Who would send you something like this?' Red asked.

'I don't know.'

'You don't know?'

'No, I was just wondering the same thing myself.'

'Wasn't there a name on the receipt?'

'It wasn't clear.'

'Take another look.'

'It's no use. All you can see is a big ink-blot.'

'You've no idea who sent it to you?'

'I can't even begin to guess.'

'Why would someone send you something like this? It's so salty and . . . well, fishy.'

'I have no idea why.'

This pointless speculation did nothing to quell Red's suspicions about the identity of the mystery sender. For Red, the most pressing question now was how to dispose of the creature.

He put on an apron, picked up a knife and, placing the eel

on a chopping board, prepared to get down to work. Unfortunately, Red had little experience in matters such as these. In the first place, the eel was far too large to fit on the chopping board. The only way to cut an eel that large without soaking it first is to place it on the floor, anchor it by the tail with one of your feet and use all your strength to cut through it.

There was a terrific thump as Red brought his knife down on the chopping board. The eel went sailing through the air and landed unscathed in the kitchen sink.

I tried to dissuade Red from his methods. 'You'll never cut it that way,' I told him. 'It's hard as a rock. You have to soak it in water before you can cut it.'

Completely ignoring my advice, Red braced himself for another try. I stood by patiently while he attempted the second cut. It ended much as I had expected, with both eel and chopping board clattering to the floor, and the eel sustaining no visible damage. Red, disheartened, set down the knife, removed his apron and went over to the kitchen sink to wash his hands. The mighty eel lay triumphant on the kitchen floor.

'What are we going to do with it?' Red asked.

Ever since I slit open the mysterious package in the post office, I had been so immersed in thoughts about the Village of Stone that I hadn't stopped to think about what I was actually going to do with the eel. Now Red's question made me remember the dried eel that hung from the rafters of my grandmother's kitchen, gathering dust, and the mouthwatering smell of my grandfather's delicious eel stew. I was determined not to be like my grandmother and waste a perfectly good eel.

'What do you mean, what are we going to do with it?' I said. 'We'll eat it, that's what! After all, it's perfectly edible.'

Red seemed to have his doubts. 'I'm having a hard time imagining putting that thing in my mouth.'

'Why? What's the problem?'

'It's like some kind of sea goblin, a big shrivelled sea goblin. I'm afraid to eat it.'

How could anyone be afraid to eat an eel? I wondered.

But Red did have a point. In a way, the eel was a sort of sea goblin. Goblins are said to be very long-lived, and eels can live for up to fifty years, sometimes even longer. What was more, this one had travelled from the depths of the East China Sea overland to a city one thousand eight hundred kilometres away. It seemed almost a shame to eat it.

But if we weren't going to eat it, what else would we do with it? Put it on display? Prop it up on an altar like a household god and burn incense to it? Since I no longer had any connection with people who earned their living from the sea, there was no danger that I could bring them bad luck by mistreating an eel. I was determined to eat it.

'Listen,' I told Red, 'we'll soak it in tap water to wash away all the salt. Then when it's soft enough, we can cut it into chunks. If we add some water, slices of ginger and cooking wine, we can make it into a clear soup. Or we can add some potato flour and make it into a stew like the eel stew I used to eat as a kid.'

'Are you really sure it's edible?' Red sounded doubtful.

'Of course. It'll be delicious.'

'Well, at any rate, I haven't got the time to deal with it.'

Red left the kitchen and headed back to his computer, as I filled the sink with water to soak the eel.

The eel was much too large to fit into the sink, and every few hours I had to feed more of its body into the water so that all of it got a chance to soften. While I was absorbed in this task, Red stayed glued to his computer, typing up the rules and regulations for his Frisbee tournament. After he had finished doing this, he designed a scorecard to keep track of points and began planning the schedule, practice locations and team assignments for the upcoming season. For Red, when it came to Frisbee, there was always work to be done.

The tournament would be held in the autumn, in the Fragrant Hills west of Beijing. It would be open to expatriates who had lived in Beijing for at least one year and to Chinese who had lived abroad for at least one year. I didn't quite understand the logic of this, but Red explained that these types of people were 'floaters' well suited to playing an airborne sport. They were also more likely than most to be able to afford the tournament and practice fees. Free-spirited by nature, they possessed the right personality type for Frisbee. I had no way to check the veracity of this claim, but Red firmly believed that the idea was the most innovative aspect of his tournament. He was trying to come up with an interesting name for the tournament or, better yet, a catchy slogan. 'Flight is Elsewhere', 'The High Life' and 'Catch!' were just a few of the slogans he was considering.

After I had finished watching the evening news, I went into the kitchen to change the eel's water. I filled the sink with fresh water and went back into the living room.

'Do you know what I hate the most?' Red asked, swivelling around to look at me.

The question caught me slightly off guard. 'No, what? Salted fish?' I assumed that Red was referring to the stench still lingering in our flat, but he shook his head.

'Um . . . the smell of salted fish?' I asked, expanding on my earlier guess.

'No, actually the smell's not that bad. It's sort of like . . .'

'Like what?'

'Like a woman's vagina.'

Ah-ha. What could I say to that?

'What I mean is, once you get used to the smell, it's really not all that bad.'

'Then what is it you hate? Living on the ground floor of a twenty-five-storey block of flats?' I figured this must be what Red hated most, but he declined to comment.

'So, tell me,' I asked impatiently.

'Ten-pin bowling!' Red proclaimed.

'Why bowling?' I had never heard Red mention that he hated bowling. What was so bad about bowling?

'Because it's loud, smoky, claustrophobic, middle-aged and boring.'

I had no idea what the man was talking about.

'Think about it. You throw a Frisbee; it flies through the open air. But in bowling, all you do is drop the ball and wait for it to roll along the ground. Frisbee is played out in the open, somewhere outdoors with grass and sky. But bowling is played in a big dark alley with bad air and a whole crowd of other people crammed inside. You have to stay in your own lane and use a big, heavy ball that rumbles down the alley like a freight train. It's loud and obnoxious. What kind of sport is that? Bowling isn't a sport – it's the anti-sport!'

Red obviously had vehement feelings on the subject. I wondered what had provoked such a hatred for bowling.

He was probably right, I reflected, but after all, bowling was just another game. If you didn't like the game, you didn't have to play it, but it certainly wasn't worth hating. These were the thoughts that ran through my head, though I did not bother to articulate them.

Sensing my lack of enthusiasm for a discussion of the comparative merits of Frisbee and bowling, Red dropped the subject. He turned back to his computer, and was soon immersed in the minutiae of his Frisbee scorekeeping system.

That's just the kind of person that Red is.

He has a certain sort of alien logic, although exactly which brand of extra-terrestrial thought it represents, I couldn't really say.

All that night I was troubled with dreams in which I was fighting the Eel Demon with a sword. I woke feeling as tired as if I had actually done battle. I couldn't remember who had won in the end.

As soon as I was dressed I went to check on the eel. Soaking in water overnight had left it soft and pliable. The tail that had protruded so rigidly yesterday now lay coiled gently around the sink. The salt that had bleached the eel's skin a ghastly white had dissipated, returning the eel to its original dark greyish hue. I carefully rejoined the two strips of eel to make it whole again, and tried to imagine what it must have looked like when it was alive. Fearsome and powerful, it had ruled the depths of the sea until it had had the misfortune to get caught in the nets of fishermen even more fearsome and powerful than itself.

As I watched the eel floating in the sink, undulating on ripples of water, I thought how alive it looked, as if it had just awakened from a long night's slumber. I stroked the eel's smooth, velvety skin and examined its long tail-fin, and tried to recall some of the traditional eel recipes from my home town. I remembered the bowls of starchy eel stew that the villagers ate at Lunar New Year and during the seventh and eighth moons. The villagers would chop water chestnuts into thin slices and add them to the stew once it was boiling. Why water chestnuts, I wondered, and not something else? Maybe it was because water chestnuts acted to reduce phlegm. The Village of Stone was so damp and dreary that most of the fishermen suffered from coughs and phlegm. Water chestnuts not only helped to clear the lungs but also made the stew taste better. As well as the water chestnuts, the villagers used shredded ginger and shallots to flavour the stew. Were those all the ingredients, or had I forgotten something? I racked my brains trying to think if there was some important step to the recipe that I had missed. Did I need aniseed, maybe, or cinnamon? When should I add the cooking wine, and how much white vinegar should I use? I started to salivate just thinking about the delicious stew, but I was worried that I might not be able to find all of the ingredients. Potato flour was available in any supermarket, but I wasn't sure whether I could buy water chestnuts at this time of year. My enthusiasm somewhat dampened, I decided that I would have to go back to my original plan and make something simpler, a clear soup perhaps.

Having made my decision, I drained the remaining water from the sink and rummaged around for a large cooking pot and some ginger.

I took my time slicing the ginger. It was fresh ginger, pale yellow and pungent. The building was so silent that you could hear each quiet crunch of the knife as it sliced through the crisp ginger. I wondered: had the person who sent me the package even stopped to consider that I might not know how to cook an eel?

Later, at lunchtime, when I placed a bowl of steaming eel soup in front of Red, I realised that it didn't matter if I hadn't got the perfect ingredients, the soup would be delicious anyway. Although Red said nothing, I could see that he was impressed. Now I cook him eel almost every day in the hope that he will come to understand a little of my past.

9

In the days that followed my grandfather's suicide, I nearly forgot all about the existence of the village mute. I spent hours every day within the confines of our house, helping my grandmother sort through my grandfather's belongings. There was nothing of any particular value, just empty bottles of spirits, discarded packets of cigarettes, empty boxes of sweet green bean cakes and several dozen Cultural Revolution-era Chairman Mao badges pinned to a strip of red cloth. Although there was no real use for any of these things, to my grandmother, everything in that room was entirely new. After all, she had not climbed up to the third floor in twenty or thirty years. It was as if my grandfather's scant few possessions – his bedclothes, pillow, cloth shoes and traditional cotton robe – could provide my grandmother with a better understanding of the man he had once been. My grandmother said that next year during the Festival of Pure Brightness, we would burn these things as offerings for my grandfather to use in the afterworld.

The second-floor room was silent and empty now. When my grandfather disappeared, so did his footsteps, the sound of his coughing, the clinking of his bottles of spirits. When everything had been removed from the room, my grandmother fastened the little window with the ocean view, so that even the sound of the sea was gone. It was the end of an era.

Several days later, I descended the stairs and went outside onto the street. It was just before the summer typhoons, and I had a vague feeling of dread. I decided I had to go and find Boy Waiting immediately and ask her father to take me out on his fishing boat. I knew that the fishermen did not usually allow women on their boats because they believed it would bring bad luck or cause the boat to capsize or run aground, but I thought it would be all right because I was still a child. I would swear to the Captain that I wouldn't bring him any bad luck.

I walked over to Boy Waiting's house next door. Neither Boy Waiting nor her mother seemed to be at home, but I saw her grandmother sitting in the courtyard, shelling shrimp. I tried calling Boy Waiting's name, but there was no answer. Her grandmother, who was completely deaf, did not hear a thing. She kept her head lowered and continued plucking the heads from the shrimp until she finally noticed me standing in the courtyard.

She informed me in a loud voice, 'Boy Waiting went to the village clinic with her mother. Her mother's just had another baby girl!'

I stood under the branches of the withered jasmine tree and tried to digest this surprising news.

As if by way of explanation, Boy Waiting's grandmother expanded on her earlier statement, 'Another useless girl!'

The world moved on so quickly. My grandfather had died, and Boy Waiting had a new baby sister. This meant that the family now had eight daughters, and that Boy Waiting had failed to bring them their long-awaited son. I wondered if her father would beat her for the failure.

I left Boy Waiting's courtyard and began wandering down Pirate's Alley. A gust of salty sea air swept through the alley like the tail of a dragon. When I reached the third turn, I gave a cold shiver. There, standing right in front of me, was the mute.

And afterwards . . . and afterwards . . .

When I ran into the mute that day, in a corner of Pirate's Alley, I imagined that it would be the same as all the previous times. He would touch me with his hand, that hand with the enormous black birthmark, he would put his fingers inside me. I

74

would feel the same terror and shame that I had before, but eventually someone would walk by and put an end to the incident. I never expected that this time would be much, much worse. The mute pointed down one of the alleyways adjacent to Pirate's Cove. He kept pointing in that direction, but I had no idea what he was trying to say. He began to make strange noises in his throat and to point even more agitatedly. I was terrified. My limbs would not obey my commands, but eventually, for some strange reason, I began to walk in the direction he was pointing. As I moved like an automaton along Pirate's Alley, it gradually dawned on me that the mute was taking me to his house. It was a house on one of the streets that adjoined Pirate's Alley, a house I never knew existed.

The mute forced me into his house and quickly kicked the door shut with his heel. Inside it was very dark. Too late, I realised that I was in great physical danger. I don't know if it was fear of physical hurt or fear of death, but at last, I regained my voice and began screaming at the top of my lungs. At first I screamed for my grandmother. When I realised how futile that was, I screamed for Boy Waiting's mother, but the mute quickly clamped a hand over my lips and silenced me by stuffing a rag into my mouth. Then he threw me onto the bed, which was as hard as a wooden board. After that, there was only excruciating pain. I was seven years old. I had no idea what was being done to my body.

If it were possible to measure death against pain, then the pain I endured in that room must have been equal to a hundred deaths. I know I must have died a hundred times that day.

I have no idea how long I was unconscious. It may have been four hours, a day or even two days later that I finally regained consciousness. When I came to, I saw that my thighs were covered with blood and that the straw mat on which I was lying was stained with congealed blood. I could not remember who I was or which road I had come by, whether I had ever had a mother or father or whether I had been born like this, lying here on this bed. I looked around at the unfamiliar room, at the stove without a shrine to the Sea Goddess and at the terrifying shadows flickering over the naked body of the man next to me, and I began to cry. My tears fell onto my body, mingling with the dried clots of blood that had formed on my skin. Even now, I still remember the dampness, the bitter taste in my mouth, the awful stench of blood. It was the smell of death, the same odour that I had smelled on my grandfather's pillow.

The room was filthy, the rafters covered with cobwebs. I noticed that there was no yellow talisman pasted on the door to ward off evil spirits. The only light in the room came from one small shuttered window set high in the wall. There were no ocean sounds, no tides, no winds or waves to be heard. It was a place very much like hell.

Into this hell walked the mute's parents. Tied to one corner of the bed, I watched as his white-haired father came into the room. He looked terribly haggard, not at all like a fisherman. He glanced at me silently, shook his head and left the room without saying a word. Some time later, the mute's mother entered the room. When she looked at me, her expression was as terrified as mine. As she left the room, followed by her son, I noticed that she was trembling. She wore her hair in the familiar style of the fishermen's wives: a chignon tied with a red ribbon and ornamented with a spray of white gardenia. What was a woman like that doing in this place? I couldn't understand how the mute could have a mother and a father. How could a monster like that have two perfectly normal parents? Was the mute really like everyone else in the village, born of a woman who wore her hair twisted into a chignon decorated with a white gardenia? How was that possible?

Shortly after the old woman left, I heard the sound of the mute breaking things in the next room. He was making a strange animal howling in the back of his throat, like a muzzled lion trying to roar. Through the open door, I could see him gesticulating wildly at his poor parents, his fingers gnarled with the effort. These were the same two hands that had invaded my body, that had taken control of my body as if they held some absolute authority over it.

Although both of the mute's parents knew what was happening, they never set foot in the room again. I remained bound to a corner of the bed. My pain was an ocean, a boundless sea whose waters stretched to the very ends of the earth. Pain was a tide crashing onto the reef, spreading across the beach, being absorbed into the sand only to emerge once more, flowing back into an endless sea. It was a tide that never ran dry. Although the mute's mother and father were still in the house, I knew that he had brought me here for a reason: he knew that his parents would protect him.

Again and again, the mute's body invaded mine. Sometimes it happened late at night, in darkness so total you could not even see your hand in front of your face. Sometimes it was in the early hours just before dawn, or at some indeterminate hour of sunlight. When I awoke from my pain-filled haze, I would strain my ears, listening for village sounds. I kept hoping that someone would pass by the house, that I would hear the footsteps of one of the villagers carrying water on a shoulder pole, the click of heels on cobblestones, or that my grandmother, calling me to dinner, would come looking for me. But I heard nothing but the wind gusting over the rooftops and the sound of tiny pebbles rolling from the tiles and onto the ground. It felt as if the house were located somewhere far outside the Village of Stone, in some distant underworld. As my hopes of rescue faltered, I began to wish that the village would be hit by a furious typhoon, a storm with winds and rain that would sweep into the Village of Stone, destroying everything in its path. I wanted everything destroyed: the mute, myself, this worthless body, this body that did not seem to be under my own control, this body that, even if I were some day to escape from this living hell, was already beyond redemption. But I knew that there would be no typhoon, no rescue nor anything else. I remained curled in a foetal position, gazing through the high window at a small, gloomy patch of sky.

Several days later, I heard voices and an unusual amount of activity going on outside the house. I had no way of knowing whether it was a festival, a funeral procession, a temple fair or some other event of celebration or mourning. I tried to cry out, but the rag stuffed into my mouth made it impossible. The mute became terribly agitated, as if he were afraid of being discovered. Even when the noise had passed, he continued to look anxious. Later that night I watched him pacing nervously around his room. After he had walked back and forth several times, he began stamping his feet on the earth floor, as if he were trying to figure out where the ground was softest. Then he dragged the bed with me on it over to the other side of the room and went out. When he returned, he was carrying a shovel and a large sack. He tossed the sack onto the floor, took up the shovel and began to dig a hole in the floor. Bit by bit, he expanded the hole in the ground, tossing shovelfuls of earth into the sack. He continued to dig as if his hands, those terrible hands with the enormous black birthmark, would never tire. When he had filled the sack, he went outside to empty it. Now and then he would stop to take a drink of water or sit down on the bed to catch his breath before resuming his digging. After two days, he seemed satisfied with the pit he had dug. He untied me from the bed, bound my hands and feet and placed me in it. Then he moved the bed back over the hole. It was a darkness blacker than death.

Now no one would ever discover the mute's secret. No one would ever discover my buried shame.

For days I drifted in and out of consciousness. Sometimes the mute would come down to me and there would be pain, but mostly I was alone. I remember being given bread and water. The mute would take the rag out of my mouth and untie my hands. Then he would pass me down the food. He was keeping me alive, although only just. Even on the brink of death, I remember feeling a powerful will to survive. Even after my tears had run dry, even after I had lost what little was left of my humanity, the only thing I wanted to do was survive.

Suddenly, I felt the sun shining down upon me. The light was blinding, and I found myself on a sandy beach. But how had I managed to crawl out of that hole in the ground? Hadn't the mute tied me up before he put me into the pit? Yet I felt no pain and it was easier to breathe. The sky seemed incredibly high, and the nearby rocks, towering and craggy, looked very much like those on the far side of the mountain of the Village of Stone. The fishermen's wives along the beach looked familiar and yet enormous, as if they had grown to the size of giants. I lowered my head to look at myself and wondered, *Is this really me?* I hardly recognised myself. When had my hands grown so hairy? And stranger still, why were they so hard and spiny? I tried to spread my hands but found that I no longer had any fingers. They were like tentacles . . . no, not tentacles but claws. I used my claws to feel around on my back and found there a hard shell, large enough to contain my entire body. I realised I was a hermit crab. I saw that the tide was rising, flooding up onto the beach. Fearing that I would be washed away, I tucked my head into my shell-house and used my claws to block the entrance. When the tide had receded and all was safe again, I poked my head out of my shell and saw that the sand stretched far away in all directions. How wonderful, I finally had my very own shell! I stretched out my claws, which grew from all sides of my body. I began to wonder: was my shell big enough? Perhaps I had grown too large for it? Wasn't that an even larger shell lying over there on the beach?

Hoping to find an even more comfortable house for myself, I began to crawl across the beach towards the larger shell. But as I drew closer, I noticed that the larger shell was not in fact a shell at all, but a hand, a hand with a large black birthmark. It was the mute's hand! Oh god, did that mean that the mute was here? But he never came out onto the beach. What was he doing here? The mute began to walk towards me very slowly.

I watched his feet move closer and closer, then come to a stop right next to me. He kicked me with his toe, but I did not even bother to curl back up into my shell because I didn't think he would be able to recognise me. He stood there for a long while, gazing at me suspiciously. Oh no, had he recognised me? No, no . . . he couldn't have. I'm not Little Dog, I'm not Coral, I'm a hermit crab. See? I'm just a little hermit crab. I tried to curl my head and body back inside my shell, but something was wrong. Oh god, what was happening to me? My shell seemed to have cracked. It was him, he, he . . . stepped on my shell and broke it and now my house had collapsed and I had nowhere else to live. I found myself being thrown into a damp, dark place, but it wasn't a shell at all, no, it felt more like a hole in the ground . . .

I have no idea how much time passed, but one day the mute forgot to retie my hands after he had fed me. Later, I heard a glass bottle crashing to the floor and, before long, the sound of snoring and a door banging open in the wind. I realised that the mute must be drunk. That was the day I made my escape from his house. I escaped with only my bloodstains, my bruises and my scars.

Once more I found myself on the cobbled streets of the Village of Stone, once more I saw the tides surging back and forth along the coast. The landscape was the same, but I was a stranger to this place. I slowly walked the length of Pirate's Alley. The alley was so narrow that only a thin ribbon of sky remained visible overhead. As I walked, I gradually began to regain my memory, slowly began to recognise this place, this familiar stretch of sea. I wondered whether the sea still recognised me.

Do you remember me, sea, do you remember this barefoot seven-year-old girl? Will you take me back, bruises and all, will you accept this little girl who has crawled out of a hole in the ground? If you will still have me, if you will let me walk silently along your shores and look upon you as I once did, if you will let me watch your sunrises and sunsets, see the tangled fishing nets and inky seaweed along your shores, I promise never to leave you again, though I grow as old as my grandmother, though my back grow bent with age.

Can you hear me, sea, tides, reefs along the shore, sand crabs crawling on the beach, can you hear what I'm saying to you? I'm begging you to listen, because besides you, there is not a single person in this world I can talk to. There is no one else I can tell my story to, not even my grandmother. All I want is to be with you, just sea and tides, no pain, no death, just you, for ever and ever and ever . . .

IO

Whenever Red and I are feeling unhappy or have just had a fight, we go to the zoo to gaze at animals even more miserable than ourselves.

Red and I like to vary the times we visit the zoo. Morning, noon, late afternoon and evening, winter, spring, summer and autumn, they all provide different opportunities for watching those sad animals in their cages. We never pay for tickets because we don't consider ourselves to be tourists; we are simply two people who have just had a fight. Sometimes we slip into the small alley hidden between the zoo and the Purple Bamboo Park and clamber over a series of small hills, unknown to most people, and down a slope that leads directly to the zoo's tiger enclosure. Sometimes we climb over the chain link fence of the Russian restaurant beside the zoo.

Every time we visit the zoo after one of our fights, we notice that the animals look even lonelier than they did the last time. It is more than loneliness; the animals have no purpose in life, nothing at all to do with their time. As soon as they are hungry, their keepers toss chunks of raw meat or pre-prepared foodstuffs into their cages. The keepers seem to think that letting wild animals go hungry is dangerous, particularly when there are small children about, so the animals have grown used to relying on handouts from humans. They have completely forgotten that their ancestors were once hunters, roaming free. Now they live in surroundings designed for them by human beings, and never have to fend for themselves. In hot weather or in cold, their keepers are always there to adjust the temperature to a more comfortable setting. It is a world in which there is no competition and no survival of the fittest, a world in which every animal seems to be playing the part, albeit rather grudgingly, of a 'kept' plaything, a stuffed animal to be petted and fed and put on display. And though they are surrounded by an elaborately artificial nature – chlorine-scented rivers and lakes, outcroppings of rocks and exotic trees transported from afar – the animals seem to have no idea what to do with their time. They stay within the confines of their respective, differently sized cages. Now and then one of the animals utters a plaintive roar, though at other times they cannot even be bothered to muster a growl. They simply gaze with tired eyes at the crowds of curious human onlookers who surround them.

Every time Red and I visit these animals, creatures even more pitiful than ourselves, we resolve not to fight again. Let's try to get along, we say to each other. Let's just try to get along. At least we do not have to live every day of our lives surrounded by metal bars.

Sometimes, at the weekend, when I am not working or when we are so bored that we cannot even be bothered to fight, Red and I spend all day sitting on one of the zoo's stone benches, drinking soda pop and watching the animals. We have discovered that the animals – elephants, giraffes, peacocks, dolphins, even squirrels – appear different, depending on the time of day and time of year. For example, on summer days when the animals are roasting like meat buns in a bamboo steamer, the zoo is completely silent. It is a silence that seems to conceal some murderous intent. The animals are listless and tired, the sunlight blinding, the heat oppressive. The tigers stay hidden in their dens and the lions skulk beneath outcroppings of rocks. Now and then a throaty growl echoes from the cool shade of their caves. The monkeys that can usually be seen climbing back and forth between the trees are deceptively calm on days like this; they perch like birds among the thick foliage. The leopards, famed for their speed and usually so alert, hang from the boughs of trees like shrivelled fruit. When they open their mouths to roar, they end up sounding like old men coughing up phlegm. It is as if the oppressive heat afflicts every animal in the zoo with a bad case of senile dementia. But on autumn mornings, the zoo seems to regain its spirit and sense of vitality. Animal voices rise and fall, as if the sound were a baton being passed from one cage to the next in some zoo-wide relay race. It begins with the tigers, pacing proudly through their dens. When the tigers finish it is the lions' turn. Their roaring infects the water buffalo and then the toads, so that soon the entire pond is seething with sound and activity. Even the peacocks in their grove respond by prancing about and unfurling their colourful plumage. Here in the zoo, in the midst of all this animal activity, Red and I finally realise our true identities. We are human beings, after all. Human beings in a zoo, that is.

And yet we are still alone, left with nothing but our own shadows. Of all the creatures in the zoo, we are the frailest.

It is a shame that the zoo has none of the sea animals or fish that I knew from the Village of Stone. There are none of the familiar starfish, eels, sharks, sea pricks or little shellfish that we called 'Buddha Hands' because they looked like the folded hands of a praying Buddha. The zoo holds no ocean, no waves, no danger.

Today, as Red and I stand by the monkey enclosure watching a mother monkey grooming her baby, I start to think about starfish. I love starfish, particularly the large, brilliantly coloured reddish-orange starfish that we had in the Village of Stone. At each low tide, starfish would appear on the beach, blossoming here and there like so many tiny flowers. Perhaps what I like most about the starfish is that, beneath its quiet, elegant exterior, it is in fact a deadly killer. The starfish is the ultimate beautiful con man. It is hard to imagine that such an adorable creature could be capable of stalking and devouring much larger prey, swallowing them whole, gulping down legions of clams, soft-bodied shellfish and small fish. A starfish will even eat its own young, not to mention its parents, grandparents and other more senior members of the family, swallowing them into its gaping, star-shaped maw. Starfish are creatures completely devoid of emotion; their only instinct is to feed on other life forms, to swallow anything and everything. Starfish have no loyalty; they recognise neither kith nor kin, and so possess exactly the sort of thick-skinned character to which I, Coral Jiang, have always aspired. From the day that my grandfather nicknamed me 'Little Dog', I think that it has always been my dream to be like one of those reddish-orange starfish, to possess no feelings, no memory and no pain. Even if I were to feel pain, as a starfish, I would at least be able to devour my own kind.

I understand starfish instinctively, in the same way that I understand the Village of Stone.

Starfish are eternally whole. Though they may lose a limb, they are echinoderms and have great regenerative powers. If any of their five limbs is severed, they have the means to grow a new one, unlike human beings for whom the loss of an arm or a leg spells permanent disability and societal discrimination. The starfish can replace the organs within a limb, and thus create a new, working limb. When a fish or shark bites into a starfish, the threatened limb simply detaches, allowing the starfish to leave the hungry predator with one of its tiny legs and make its escape with the other four intact. Until its death, a starfish always preserves its dignity and grace. How much better it would be if human beings could be more like starfish.

I am so immersed in my own idle thoughts that I scarcely notice Red talking to me.

'We should get a dog. What do you think?'

I shake my head.

'What are you afraid of? It's not as if we're talking about having a child.'

'It's still a lot of trouble.'

'Trouble is what life is all about!'

I shake my head again.

'If we had a dog, Coral, you wouldn't be lonely.'

'Our flat is too small for a dog.'

'That's true. What if we get a cat instead?' Red suggests. 'Cats don't need as much room.'

'No, that's no good either. Cats have too much *yin*, too much dark matter and negative energy. It would be like having another woman around.'

'What's wrong with that? You'd have another woman around the house to keep you company.'

'Why do we have to get a pet? I don't feel like looking after anything right now.'

'Why not?'

'Because it's too much trouble.'

'Pets are not just about trouble. A pet can play with you, too.'

'You mean I'd have to play with *it*.'

We are silent for a moment.

'Red, I don't want a pet.'

'That's because you only love yourself.'

'I love you, too.'

I sound so hesitant. I can hear it as soon as the words are out of my mouth, and it makes me wish I hadn't said anything at all.

'You don't understand what love is.' I hear the disappointment and loss in Red's voice.

The mother monkey and her baby have stopped swinging through the trees and are nestled in the fork of one of the branches. The mother monkey picks the lice from her baby's fur and, with one hairy paw, pops them into her mouth. I wonder: *Is this love, or simple hunger?*

'You say you love me, but I don't feel it.'

As he speaks, Red gazes at the two monkeys. The wind ruffles the leaves of the tree. The monkeys rouse themselves from their perch, swing through the branches of the trees and disappear from sight.

11

In the days I had disappeared into the mute's house, my grandmother's hair had gone completely white.

Her hair had always been sprinkled with white, and she wore
it in a coil secured with a silver hairpin. But by the time I
escaped from the mute's house and returned to my grandmother's home, it had turned as white as snow. She looked like
an old madwoman.

She said she searched everywhere for me.

She said she thought that I must have been swept away by
the Sea Demon.

But the Sea Demon never took children with nicknames like
Dog. The Sea Demon didn't want children like me, children
cursed by fate.

She said she thought I had disappeared like my father, fated
never to return.

She said she thought my grandfather, now an angry ghost,
had spirited me away to join him in the underworld, depriving
her of her one and only hope.

She said she thought that I must have committed some offence
in a previous life, some wrongdoing that I was being punished
for in this life.

When she laid eyes on me again, all she could do was to
repeat, 'So the Sea Demon didn't want you . . . the Sea Demon
didn't want you after all . . .'

It was as if I had become a mute myself. I could say nothing,
for I knew that the moment I opened my mouth, I would be
devoured by shame. All I could do was hug my grandmother

tightly and cry. My grandmother cried with me. Her body felt so frail and emaciated, so terribly small.

I believe in retribution. The Village of Stone taught me that retribution awaits us all. I would have my retribution sooner than expected. The mute would die.

He died that same year, during the most destructive typhoon to hit the Village of Stone in decades.

The typhoon tore the roof from his house, causing the entire structure to come tumbling down. He and his elderly parents died a horrible death, crushed beneath an avalanche of ceramic roof tiles. The same typhoon caused some of the other houses along the shore to collapse as well, killing several other villagers. After the typhoon had passed, dozens of neighbours helped to dig the bodies from beneath the collapsed beams. After a full day of digging, they had pulled five or six bodies from the rubble.

The bodies were the main topic of dinner table conversation in the village for several days afterwards. After the typhoon season ended, however, the villagers never brought the subject up again.

And so it was that the death of the mute left no real lasting impression on the Village of Stone.

Each time I passed the alley where the mute had lived, I would stop and stare at the piles of rocks and baked clay tiles still littering the ground where his house had stood. I felt dazed, unsure what to do or which way to turn. The man whose death I had desired so long had, one day, simply been buried under a pile of debris. I was free to walk along the beach again, free to wander up and down the length of Pirate's Alley. Never again would anyone follow, threaten or coerce me. Yet suddenly I found myself with no idea where to go or what to do. I spent my days accompanying my grandmother to the Temple of the Sea Goddess on the mountaintop, where I wandered around, watching my grandmother burn incense and recite her sutras for hours on end. Her monotonous chanting, in time to the beating of the wooden fish drums, reverberated through the temple. Life seemed so terribly lonely, like a single blade of yellowed grass growing on the dry, barren mountaintop of the Village of Stone.

12

Beijing continues rumbling along. With each new day, the city seethes. As the scaffolding of newly constructed skyscrapers rises ever upward, well into the path of low-flying aircraft, Red and I remain huddled here on the ground floor.

If there is any cause for celebration amidst all this, it is that our rent, at least, has not been raised.

A new tenant is moving into Number 205, the flat directly above ours.

For the past few days, we have listened to a steady stream of things being removed from Number 205, major items such as refrigerators, washing machines and large wardrobes scraping loudly across the floor. Number 205 must be a real treasure trove, for the removal has been going on for three full days. We have had to turn our television set up to the highest volume just to drown out the clamour. Our television now squawks from morning until night, giving us a steady diet of China Central Television – early morning newscasts, English tutorials, Beijing Opera, Chinese cooking shows, programmes on artificial insemination, talk shows, assertiveness courses for modern women, live news coverage and late night weather reports.

Red, upon returning home from buying some frozen dumplings, informs me of the latest development: the tenant from 205 has finally finished moving things out and now the new tenant has arrived. He excitedly describes the scene outside. 'It's a woman with bleached blonde hair, I mean really, really platinum blonde hair, with big permanent waves. She's wearing one of those tight leopard-print dresses, you know the kind I mean, very low-cut. Judging from her furniture, she must have loads of money. She's got a red leather sofa – at least I think it's real leather – and a big flat-screen television set, at least twice the size of ours. The old woman who operates the lift kept looking the blonde up and down, like she was sizing her up or something. Then the old lady told her that she couldn't allow her to tie up the lift moving her furniture, so she had to use the stairs instead. But the men from the moving company said that they preferred using the stairs anyway because it was less trouble . . .'

Red talks much the way a sailor, away at sea for five long months, might describe the sudden appearance of a naked blonde mermaid in the middle of the ocean.

'Well, she certainly does sound like a bombshell.' I am tempted to run outside myself to see if I can catch a glimpse of this woman. After all, we are going to be neighbours.

I pick up the rubbish bag on the way out, and walk to the main entrance of our building. The front gate is blocked by a large, rather decrepit removals van. Two removals men in filthy uniforms are busy lifting a large dining table from the van. The same group of old men who always seem to be squatting outside our building playing chess have stopped their game and turned to stare at the woman. They seem to be enjoying the peep show. As for the woman, she is exactly as Red described her. She has curly platinum blonde hair, bright red lipstick, a tight-fitting leopard-print dress and a wide leather belt slung around her hips. With her stiletto heels and silk stockings completing the ensemble, the effect is indeed overwhelming. Even more so is the way she carries herself. Hers is not the attitude of someone living on the first floor; it is the attitude of someone looking down upon the world from high atop the penthouse suite. She stands amongst the dirty rubbish bins, clutching a cat with fur the exact shade of her hair. She and the cat, watching the movers' progress, seem to exude the very same air of indifference.

★　　★　　★

With the addition of this woman to our daily lives, Red and I find our range of conversational topics greatly enriched.

The noises begin at about noon. They start in her bathroom, when the sound of running water upstairs begins to reverberate through the pipes in our own bathroom. From that point, there is no silence to be had. We hear her footsteps on the floor above us, tap tap tapping to the sound of some percussion-heavy music such as rock or disco. We cannot tell whether she is dancing or doing exercises. Although we have seen her in person and know that she is not at all overweight, just extremely voluptuous, every time she jumps up and down, it sets the ceiling of our flat shaking. The impact causes the tassels on our hanging lamp to swing back and forth as if we are experiencing a minor earthquake. After she has finished with her aerobics or exercises, the music stops and her phone begins ringing. By late afternoon, we can hear the constant opening and closing of her front door, suggesting a steady stream of visitors. We are able to infer something about the nature of her guests by the sound of their laughter, their coughing, sneezing, heavy footsteps and the type of music playing on the stereo. Judging by these and by the volume and pitch of the guests' voices, we deduce that her visitors are exclusively male. Having reached this interesting conclusion, Red and I sit in our flat quietly eating our dinner of frozen, pre-prepared foodstuffs: Auntie Su's Frozen Wonton, Little Miss Zang Frozen Dumplings and Even-the-Dog-Won't-Eat-'Em Savoury Buns. As my dinner settles in my stomach, I imagine a crowd of male guests crammed into that tiny flat, clustered around the curly-haired blonde in the tight leopard-print dress.

At night, I lie awake on our mattress, so close to the ground that I can hear the earth's heartbeat, see the tiny ants crawling up the base of the bedside lamp. The sounds of the woman's lovemaking seems to travel a direct line to our flat, carrying down through the ceiling and into our mundane lives. Sometimes it is the sound of a headboard banging up against the wall, steadily, rhythmically, as if a carpenter has taken up a hammer and is driving nails into the wall. Other times it is simply the sound of two bodies falling off the bed and onto the ground. As the bodies roll around the floor, I can distinguish sounds of an elbow being propped up, a knee banging on the ground, a complex change of position. The woman's cries are occasionally muffled, as if a hand has been clamped over her mouth. Sometimes it is hard to tell whether I am listening to lovemaking or fighting.

During the day, our high-rise building is more powerful than our blonde neighbour. Her private life has to compete with the wholesome lives contained within these twenty-five storeys, lives filled with domestic trivia and household gossip, husbands telling wives about their day at work, children telling parents about their day at school and old women telling old men about their day spent playing mah-jong. The life of a woman whose sole agenda is her body seems to pale somewhat in the midst of this larger society.

But in the hours after midnight, the woman's vitality bursts forth, as she makes love with amazing stamina. Sometimes she falls to giggling so hard that she can hardly catch her breath. Each night, I accompany her midnight song until at last, late at night, she falls into a deep and silent sleep.

In the small hours of the morning I lie awake thinking about the day Boy Waiting's younger sister was swept away.

After giving birth to Boy Waiting, her mother began to lose faith in her ability to produce a son, but her mother-in-law urged her to keep trying. Boy Waiting's grandmother believed that the more sons and grandsons a family had, the more prosperous it would be. Then there was the matter of the family's fishing boat. Without a son, who would take over the boat when the Captain grew too old to sail? Hoping for a son, however, continued to prove much easier than producing one. Even the most casual observer could see that the house was filled with women — seven daughters, their mother and grandmother. That added up to nine hungry mouths to feed, and not one of them was a sea scavenger. The family needed another fisherman if it hoped to feed all those girls. It was not enough to rely on the old Sea Captain, for nobody knew whether or when he might meet with an accident at sea. For a fisherman, each voyage could prove to be his last. To stave off this eventuality, Boy Waiting's grandmother walked to the temple on the far side of the mountain every day to make offerings and burn incense. She managed to walk surprisingly fast for a woman with such small, bound feet. When she reached the temple, she offered incense to both Guanyin and the Sea Goddess, praying to the Sea Goddess for the Captain's safe return and to Guanyin that her daughter-in-law might bear a grandson.

Though the Captain placed no blame on his wife, he must have felt entitled to at least one son, a boy to take his place on the fishing boat. I never saw the Captain worship anyone or anything, but when he drank, he drank like religion, tossing back one large bowl of wine after another in the manner of a man worshipping at the cups of the Buddhist patriarchs. I suspect that deep in his heart, the Captain still harboured hopes for a son. But when Boy Waiting's youngest sister, his eighth consecutive daughter, came into this world, the Captain lost whatever remaining faith he had in temple offerings and incense burnings. His wife's milk had finally dried up. She seemed to grow more shrivelled, as if the years of constant childbearing had left her as desiccated as a dried squid. In order to conserve her strength for work around the house and manual labour on the beach, she decided that she would have no more children.

After living with six older sisters for so many years, Boy Waiting was thrilled to have a little sister at last. The arrival of a baby sister meant that Boy Waiting was no longer the youngest child in the family, picked on by her older sisters and despised by her grandmother. It also meant that Boy Waiting finally had someone smaller than herself, someone she could push around.

Though the new baby was a girl, her parents named her Boy at Last and decided to raise her as a son. Her mother was kept busy running back and forth to the tailor's shop to have clothes made for the baby. All were shirts and shoes and little hats embroidered with leopards and tigers, boy clothes meant to transform Boy at Last into a real son. Boy at Last was the only child in the family permitted to wear a tiger hat. None of the other seven daughters had ever had one. It would have been unthinkable, because tiger hats were reserved for boys. When Boy at Last began to grow a thick head of hair, her mother took her to the barber to be given a boy's haircut. With her hair shaved on both sides and a little tuft in the middle, Boy at Last looked just like one of the cherubic little boys – often pictured riding a giant carp – on the Chinese New Year posters. From then on, Boy at Last looked and behaved just like all the other little boys in the village. She never played girls' games, and her parents spoiled her terribly. Boy Waiting was forced to suffer the double indignity of being deprived of a younger sister she could pick on and being cast as a little nursemaid to the family's eighth child, her ostensible 'younger brother'. As Boy at Last grew older, she became even more of a tomboy, crude of features and possessed of an oddly grating voice. On windless nights, the sound of Boy at Last crying was loud enough to wake everyone in the village.

My grandmother said that Boy at Last had not been much blessed in this latest incarnation. By rights, she ought to have been born male, but now she was neither male nor female. Woe to her unlucky parents.

Regardless of my grandmother's feelings on the subject, Boy at Last remained the apple of her parents' eyes.

From the time she was very small, Boy at Last accompanied us to play on the beach. She had no fear of the surf, and loved to clamber over the rocks by the seashore. She preferred to play with the boys, joining happily in their fights, spitting contests and dares to see who was brave enough to pick up a crab by its pincers. Everyone regarded her as a boy. While this tomboy sister was rough-housing on the shore with the other boys, Boy Waiting and I stood apart from them, gazing out at the ocean. It was as if their antics on the seashore had no connection with us, as if their ocean and our ocean were completely separate entities, two different facets of the Village of Stone.

There were more typhoons in the Village of Stone during the seventh moon than at any other time of year. For weeks on end, the village was struck by one typhoon after another. Typhoon rains flooded the lanes and Pirate's Alley, the longest and most winding alleyway in the village, was transformed into a raging river. When the ground floor of the houses flooded, the residents moved upstairs, lugging with them their stores of rice and flour, furniture and other belongings, even the pigs from their backyards. They set up ladders so that they could pile stones upon the tiled rooftops to keep them from being ripped off by the typhoons. Because there were frequent power cuts at night, the village headman's office issued candles to all the villagers, two packets per household. During the day, the village children went out to the flooded streets to play in the water. They fished out errant sandals, plastic bottles, rotting pieces of Tangjiu toffee, waterlogged crabs and other debris washed in from who knows where. When the children returned home, they found the adults busy making lanterns for the Festival of the Dead.

Despite the bad weather, the fishing boats in the harbour were never idle at this time of year. There was an abundance of yellow croaker, crabs, eels and butterfish to be found in the waters. Other than the early winter fishing season, it was the best catch of the year, thanks to the tropical current that flowed in from the South Pacific and mingled with another current from the north. The combined currents, one warm and one cool, brought with them an abundance of sea life. Schools of fish gathered near the shore as if for some important undersea conference. For this reason, the true fishermen of the village were more than willing to brave the risks of setting out to sea. Every year at this time, Boy Waiting's father, the Sea Captain, led a group of four or five other fishing boats out to sea for the catch.

In the early part of the seventh moon, the Village of Stone

entered into an extended period of humidity caused by typhoon rains. The damp seeped in everywhere. Rain surged down the flight of stone steps leading up to the mountain, transforming it into a white waterfall. That year, as the Captain prepared to set sail, there was neither wind nor rain. Boy Waiting's mother spent her days in the kitchen cooking ten days' worth of food for her husband to take along on his voyage. She sealed the rations in waterproof containers with an ample supply of condiments such as shrimp paste and fermented tofu. As the captain busied himself laying in a supply of matches, plastic tarpaulins, raincoats and cigarettes for his journey, he could not have imagined the implications that this trip would have for his beloved tomboy, Boy at Last. I remember standing in the courtyard that day with Boy Waiting, Boy at Last and their older sisters, watching the Captain pack the equipment he would use on his boat. When he was finished, a crowd of women including Boy Waiting's mother, her daughters and myself went down to the beach to see him off. Even my grandmother came to the beach that day. I remember her muttering that this was the Festival of the Dead, the day that the Sea Demon dragged the living down to the underworld. The fishermen were too greedy for the catch, she grumbled. They were certain to come to a bad end.

I believed my grandmother. Though she was a woman of few words, she had witnessed more than her share of deaths in the Village of Stone. The deaths that she had seen in that time probably outnumbered the sentences she had spoken.

The skies were clear for the first few days after the Captain set sail, but on the third day, a typhoon moved in. As the storms intensified, a steady stream of fishing boats began returning to port. Some had been damaged in the storms and forced to turn back before they had even reached international fishing waters; others returned with nets full of yellow croaker, butterfish and crabs. On the fourth day, a fishing boat with a torn sail returned to port bearing news of Boy Waiting's father. His boat had sailed out very far, well into international waters. The other boat had maintained voice contact with the Captain's boat for a while, but at last was forced to turn back and lost contact with him. Soon all the other boats in the village had returned to shore, but none of them brought Boy Waiting's mother any news of her Captain. She went to the beach every day at dusk to watch for her husband's boat. Sometimes she even went up to the mountaintop, but the sea was covered with an impenetrable haze, obscured by mist and driving rain. Even if there were a boat out on those waves, nobody would be able to see it.

By the fifteenth day of the seventh moon, there was still no news of the Captain. It had been over a week since he set sail, but there was no sign of his boat or of any signal lights on the water. Boy Waiting and Boy at Last accompanied their mother to the shore every day to watch for their Captain's boat. Every evening at dusk, they returned home disappointed.

At this time of the year, the beach was deserted. Because I had neither a mother nor a father waiting for me at home, I sat on the beach every day, among the unfinished piles of fishing nets, and watched Boy Waiting and her family waiting for their Captain to return. The thundering surf and ocean winds were deafening. Every now and then, in the silences between gusts of wind, I could hear the metallic jangling of the amulet Boy at Last wore around her neck, but the sound was soon carried away on the wind.

By the morning of the fifteenth day of the seventh moon, the typhoon winds had reached a crescendo, but Boy Waiting's mother told the other villagers that she was certain the Captain would be coming back soon. No matter how far he sailed, she reminded them, he always managed to return in time for the Festival of the Dead. And besides, the Captain would never allow the Sea Demon to steal his hard-won catch.

Boy Waiting's mother and her daughters spent the day of the festival making fish balls for the evening meal. By afternoon, a driving rain was falling outside, and the winds had whipped the surface of the ocean into churning waves. Boy Waiting's mother picked up some umbrellas and oilskins and told her eldest daughter, Golden Phoenix, to watch the house while she went to the beach. As she was heading out with Boy Waiting in tow, Boy at Last pleaded and whined to be allowed to go with them. In the end, her mother gave in and allowed her youngest to come along.

Struggling to keep a grip on their umbrellas, the three made their way down the windswept length of Pirate's Alley. When they reached the end, they could see nothing, for the sea was cloaked in an impenetrable haze of mist and rain. They decided to climb to the mountaintop for a better view. Boy Waiting's mother stood on the mountaintop for a very long time, holding her umbrella and gazing out to sea. The villagers who lived near the mountain said that she looked like a statue, so intense was her concentration on that grey expanse of sea. It was as if she could see all the way across the Taiwan Straits to Chinmen harbour on the opposite shore, where the mainland fishing boats sometimes took shelter from the typhoons. All the time she stood on the mountaintop, her two young children stayed by her side. Like their mother, Boy Waiting and Boy at Last were steadfast in their hope that their father would return. A person who knows hope is a person who knows happiness. I know this because from the age of seven, I lived without hope. I had no returning father upon that vast stretch of ocean. I lived each and every day beside that ocean, but to me it was nothing more than a neighbour. I lived next door to it, just as I lived next door to Boy Waiting's family. I had always known them, always understood them, but I could never be one of them. The ocean, like Boy Waiting's family, was a door through which I could never enter.

The sea was my neighbour, but it belonged to my next-door neighbour.

An hour after her ascent, Boy Waiting's mother managed to glimpse a sail on the water. It disappeared behind the waves, reappeared and then disappeared again. The sky had long since grown dark, and the rain was coming down in sheets. Between the rain falling from the sky and the surf pounding the shore, it seemed that there was nothing left in this world but water,

water, and more water. Boy Waiting's mother made her way down the mountain. To her children she said, 'You see? Didn't I say that your father would be back before the festival? He wasn't going to let that Sea Demon have his catch!' She led the two girls down to the sand, where they huddled beneath an oilcloth. Though she did her best to shield Boy Waiting and her sister from the rain with her umbrella, soon both girls were shivering and Boy at Last seemed to be in danger of being swept away by the gusting winds. Their mother regretted bringing the children to the beach, but it was too late to take them back home now. Her only choice was to take them to the marshy area near the shore, where the villagers raised seaweed. It had a small storage shed that she hoped would shelter them from the wind and rain. When they reached the shed, they found the door locked and the place deserted. Boy Waiting and Boy at Last huddled outside the shed, which was filled with fishing nets, tools and blades used to cut seaweed.

After she had settled the children safely by the shed, Boy Waiting's mother ran back down to the beach. The outline of the boat grew clearer, but it was moving very slowly. The swells on the surface of the sea rose like backdrop scenery, obscuring the tiny boat. At this point, a group of villagers carrying umbrellas and oil lanterns appeared on the beach. They were celebrating the Festival of the Dead as they did every year, drumming on metal pans with sticks to drive away the Sea Demon.

The crowd of villagers grew larger. Their lanterns were like dozens of tiny stars, casting flickering shadows on the dark, angry sea. By now, the boat was not far from shore. As Boy Waiting's mother watched it approach, she grew more and more excited. The Sea Goddess had heard her prayers and brought her Captain home safely.

The other fishermen's wives were unable to hold back any longer. They began to shout their husbands' names, hoping that the men on the boat could hear them.

Nobody paid the slightest attention to the two little girls standing in the distance near the seaweed beds.

The sound of the villagers' drumming became more muted,

and there was a pause in the howling of the wind. Boy Waiting's mother seemed to be listening to something, some sound only she could hear. It was her child crying! Her seventh daughter, Boy Waiting, was crying!

As the boat moved closer to shore, the villagers on the beach surged forward to meet it. Boy Waiting's mother left the crowd and rushed frantically towards the enormous expanse of marsh near the shoreline. Cloaked in darkness, the marsh seemed boundless, unfathomably deep. When she reached the little shed, she found it deserted. Following the direction of her child's voice, she waded deeper into the seaweed, her knees sinking into the muck. At last, she drew close enough to discern the cries more clearly. Boy Waiting was shouting her sister's name.

The little fishing boat finally reached shore, accompanied by petrol fumes from the motor and the hubbub of the villagers' voices. The Captain and his crew, exhausted after their many days battling the storms, disembarked from the boat, and their wives and families rushed forward to welcome them home. No one was in any hurry to unload the spoils from the hold of the ship. In truth, the catch was not quite as good as they had anticipated, but this was of little consequence. The most important thing was that the men had made it home safely.

When the Captain, Boy Waiting's father, set foot on the beach, he was puzzled to find neither his wife nor his children waiting for him. He circled the crowd several times, searching in vain for his family, before he finally gave up and returned to his boat. Not long afterward, as he was lowering the ship's flag from the mast and the villagers were still milling on the shore with their lanterns, there came the sound of Boy Waiting's mother wailing in the distance.

Her youngest child, her precious Boy at Last, was dead. She had drowned in the shallows just beyond the seaweed beds, less than a hundred metres from shore. Boy Waiting's mother had tried to rescue her daughter, but was hindered by the gusts of wind and rain. By the time the other adults arrived to help, it was already too late.

I heard the villagers say that when they pulled Boy at Last's body from the water, it was bloated with salt water, swollen like a fish bladder.

The Festival of the Dead was drawing to a close. Every house in the village was illuminated by the glow of home-made paper lanterns, and the last fishing boat had arrived home safely, its nets filled with yellow croaker and cuttlefish. The village was safe for another year, but the Sea Demon had managed to spirit away one of its children.

Boy Waiting's family had lost their youngest and most precious child. Once again, Boy Waiting found herself the youngest girl in a household of girls.

Boy Waiting had watched her sister die. Powerless to help, she had stood in the darkness of the marsh and watched. The long tangled strands of seaweed that the villagers cultivated along the shoreline were like wire mesh, forming an invisible netting that demarcated the boundary between the mud-flats and the sea. Boy at Last had been swept over this inky green boundary to her death. After the death of her sister, Boy Waiting seemed to grow up almost overnight. Her youthful expression gave way to a more serious expression, and she started to look just like all the other adults in the Village of Stone. I think I understand why Boy Waiting had to grow up so fast. Growing up was the only way to protect yourself from the scary things in this world. Things like shame, fear, hunger, loneliness and death.

The Captain always liked to say that there were only three inches of wooden plank separating a sea scavenger from the Sea Demon. Only this time, the Sea Demon had come not for the Captain's boat, but for one of his children.

After Boy at Last was gone, a series of other misfortunes befell the family. Boy Waiting's father was plagued with mishaps at sea: a torn sail, a damaged stern, an oil leak in a recently repaired motor. More often than not, his ship encountered typhoons and was forced to take refuge in Chinmen harbour. Just as the family seemed to be falling apart, Golden Phoenix announced that she was leaving the village. She had always been the hardest worker in the family, but now she had decided to join the provincial Shaoxing opera troupe. Not only was Golden Phoenix beautiful, she also had a lovely singing voice. Although she was not an official member of the village opera troupe, she could sing the ingénue roles better than any of the regular actresses, and even had her own silken costume and phoenix headdress. She liked to dress up as Lin Meimei, Meng Lijun and other famous characters, and could sing the lead role in *The Journey of Eighteen Li*, a classic story of two star-crossed lovers. Her parents were opposed to Golden Phoenix's joining the opera troupe because they considered acting a disreputable profession. They imagined shiftless men, women of dubious virtue, actors chasing after actresses, actresses chasing after actors and all manner of scandalous behaviour. They feared that if their daughter joined the operatic troupe, she would fall in love with some effeminate, unreliable actor and before long, the young couple would be travelling the country, putting on shows in far-flung provinces – or even worse, they would move to the big city, never to return. The Captain said that he didn't care how well those actors sang; none of them would ever be man enough to take over his fishing boat. But the Captain's words fell on deaf ears. The more he argued, the more determined Golden Phoenix was to leave the village.

As long as I can remember, Golden Phoenix had always been the most beautiful girl in the Village of Stone. She was truly extraordinary. Most of the women in the village were dark and wiry, their skin coarsened by years of exposure to the wind and sun and rain. Golden Phoenix, with her pale, delicate skin and voluptuous figure, was like a rare pearl in comparison. When she walked down the street with her procession of sisters, she looked like a swan leading a crowd of ugly ducklings. She seemed to glow, as if she emanated a natural purity and grace. When she was younger, she was voted the queen of the Weaver Goddess's Festival, held on the seventh day of the seventh moon. According to legend, it was the only day of the year when the Weaver Goddess was able to cross the skies to

meet with her beloved Heavenly Herdsman. The girl chosen as
queen represented the Weaver Goddess. On the eve of the
festival, it was traditional for the village girls to gather seven
different types of flowers and leave them outside overnight in
a courtyard or on a rooftop to 'gather the dew'. The next morning when the girls awoke, they would bathe in the fragrant dew,
said to be the tears of the Weaver Goddess and her Herdsman.
The dew bath was said to brighten the eyes and whiten the
skin. I supposed that Golden Phoenix must have taken an awful
lot of dew baths to become so beautiful.

Golden Phoenix left the village in the end, although her
father tried his best to stop her. Before she left, he called on
the provincial operatic troupe and begged them not to let her
sign up. He also paid a visit to the bus station, the only point
of exit from the village, and asked the old stationmaster not to
sell Golden Phoenix a bus ticket. I don't know whether or not
the old stationmaster agreed. As I have said, he was a very
powerful man. At any rate, Golden Phoenix somehow managed
to leave the village, and when she left, she left for good. She
ran off to join the provincial operatic troupe and was admitted
easily enough, by virtue of her natural good looks and singing
ability. After that, I never saw her again.

When she left, I was as sad as Boy Waiting. It felt as if I had
lost an older sister, too.

Golden Phoenix's departure changed the way I thought about
the Village of Stone. It made me realise that there were gaps in
the village, gaps through which people could escape. Before
Golden Phoenix left, I had thought of the village as a sealed
fortress, bordered only by an endless, impassable sea. Her departure meant that I finally had some hope of escape. But every
time I stood at the gate of the bus station and watched the
stationmaster sitting, all-powerful, behind his tiny ticket window,
my hopes began to fade. I wasn't even tall enough to reach the
ticket window. Even if I were taller, I still had no money to
pay for a ticket. I would just have to wait until I was more

grown-up. I couldn't wait to grow up, because it seemed to me that being a grown-up was the only way to resolve all my problems. If only I were grown-up, I could leave this place. I could leave behind that cruel carnivorous sea and the cobblestone alleyways where the mute had once walked.

13

I was always hoping that one day the stationmaster would speak to me.

I was always hoping that one day, he would come out from behind his ticket office window and greet me.

But the old stationmaster seemed to have grown into the Village of Stone bus station like one of the fixtures. It was as if there were some invisible thread connecting him to the book of tickets upon his desk, a thread that bound his lower body to the seat of that ravelled rattan chair and then stretched on to the three buses parked in the yard.

The stationmaster was like a seated Buddha destined to spend every second of every minute of every hour of every day safe-guarding the village bus depot.

One day, however, as I was hanging around the station gate, the stationmaster raised his head and looked at me through the dust-streaked windows of the station ticket office. Then, to my delight, he put down his blue ticket book and red stamp and came limping out towards me. He motioned for me to sit down with him on a step.

'Little Dog, that's your nickname, isn't it? What's your real name? You must have a real name, right?'

'Coral.'

'Coral Jiang?'

I nodded my head.

'Well now, that's a much prettier name than Little Dog.'

This elicited a smile from me, because I thought it was the nicest thing that anyone had ever said to me in my whole life.

At last, I began to feel happy. But suddenly, my eyes filled with tears and I felt sad again. I did not want to cry in front of the stationmaster, because I didn't want him to see how ugly I looked when I cried.

'Your grandfather's name is Jiang Mingfeng.'

I lowered my head and made no answer.

'And your father's name is Jiang Qinglin.'

I looked up at the old stationmaster in surprise, for it was a name I had never heard before.

'It's a shame, that.' He sighed. I wasn't sure on what or whose account he was sighing.

'But you know, hard luck only makes a person stronger,' he added.

I did not know whether the stationmaster was referring to me or to my father. Maybe he was talking about himself. After all, he was crippled in one leg. I wondered if his leg still hurt when he walked.

'You know that, don't you, Coral? You've had a hard time of it, but you're a survivor.'

Me? A survivor?

The three buses stood silently, parked in a neat row. Why wasn't anyone on them? Why didn't anyone want to ride those buses? If it were up to me, I'd get on one of those buses and go somewhere far away, the farther the better.

'Where do these buses go?' I finally worked up the nerve to ask.

'The other side of the mountain. The roads are so bad that they are building a tunnel, several very long tunnels in fact, to get to the other side.'

'How long are they?'

'Oh, very, very long. And they're only halfway through. There are people up there blasting tunnels every day. Eventually they'll clear away all the rocks, and it will be much easier to get to the other side.'

I raised my head. The stationmaster seemed to be talking about a place so high it was almost ethereal, some place in the infinite distance. That was the direction from which my grand-mother had arrived as a girl, when she walked all the way from her village to the sea.

'Right now all the roads are blocked with boulders that have fallen from the mountain during the blasting, so none of the buses can get through. I'm left with nothing to do. But that's all right, because it gives me the chance to talk to you.'

I made no answer, because I was busy thinking. I was hoping that they would finish the tunnels soon, so that the buses could drive out again.

Noticing my silence, the old stationmaster became thoughtful. I got the feeling that he was trying to think of something to cheer me up.

'Do you know why they call this place the Village of Stone?'

I pondered for a moment. 'Because there are a lot of stones?'

'No, because in the beginning, there weren't any stones here at all.'

My curiosity now piqued, I tried to imagine a Village of Stone without any stones.

'Have you ever heard the story of the Dragon King and the boy who boiled the sea?'

I shook my head.

'Your grandmother never told you that story?'

'My grandmother's not from around here.'

The old stationmaster nodded his head.

'Well, in the beginning this place wasn't called the Village of Stone. It was called the Village of the Marsh. It stood right on the coast and there were only a few people living here. At that time, the Dragon King of the Eastern Sea was in charge of things in the village. But life was difficult, because between the typhoons and the tides, the entire village was one big marsh-land. Fields were inundated with water and boats were washed away in the floods. Eventually someone from the village volun-teered to boil away the sea to drive out the Dragon King.'

Slowly, the old stationmaster began to warm up to his tale. 'Back in those days, everyone said that there was gold buried beneath the Village of the Marsh. Even though they knew that living in the Village of the Marsh was dangerous, greedy people from all over moved to the village to search for buried treasure. Though the people were greedy, the Dragon King of the Eastern Sea was even greedier. He decided to flood the village so that everyone would leave and he could have the buried gold all to himself. The Dragon King spent every day, from morning until night, stirring up trouble, calling on the winds and rains and tides to drive everyone out of the village. But the villagers couldn't stop thinking about all that buried gold, so they refused to leave.

'Now, near the village there was a mountain called Weaver Mountain, and on top of the mountain lived the Weaver Goddess. When she saw what was happening, she decided that she had to do something to save the lives of the villagers. So she sat at her weaving for seven thousand, seven hundred and forty-nine days and nights until she had finished weaving a golden fishing net out of nine thousand nine hundred and eighty-one pounds of golden thread. She brought the net to the Village of the Marsh and said to the villagers, "I am giving you this gift of a golden fishing net. Now you must send one of your own out to sea to do battle with the Dragon King." But the remaining villagers were money-grubbing treasure seekers only concerned with saving their own skin and all of them were too afraid to go out to sea.

'Finally, a little boy – let's call him the Sea Child – stepped forward and volunteered to take on the Dragon King. Now, the boy was still very young, only seven or eight years old, and he was still dressed in the split-bottomed trousers that babies wear, but he bravely thumped his chest and said to the villagers, "I'll do it! I'll go out to sea!" The villagers were shocked. The Weaver Goddess, however, simply chuckled and said, "You are truly a child of the sea. The golden fishing net is yours." The boy took the golden fishing net and, following the instructions of the Weaver Goddess, stood beside the sea and shouted, "Bigger!" Sure enough, the minute the boy shouted this command, muscles began to bulge under his skin and he grew taller and taller, bigger and bigger, until he was transformed into an incredibly powerful giant who towered over all the villagers. The now gigantic Sea Child easily picked up the nine thousand nine hundred and eighty-one pound golden fishing net and cast it over the ocean.

'To his surprise, the net snared one of the Dragon King's generals, the Dog-faced Eel Demon in charge of guarding the Dragon King's treasure chest. The Sea Child knew that among the many treasures in the Dog-faced Eel Demon's possession was the magical Sea-Boiling Cauldron. The Sea Child shouted "Smaller!" and the golden fishing net gradually began to shrink, trapping the Dog-faced Eel Demon inside. The Eel Demon had no choice but to surrender. When the boy had taken the Eel Demon captive, he made him open the Dragon King's Chest of One Hundred Treasures and hand over the magical Sea-Boiling Cauldron. The Sea Child set the cauldron on the beach as the Weaver Goddess had told him to do, filled it with sea water and set a blazing fire underneath. Soon the water in the cauldron was bubbling and boiling. On and on the water bubbled. A few minutes passed, and the boy saw steam begin to rise from the surface of the ocean. After another few minutes, the boy saw that the surface of the ocean had turned a fiery red. Another few minutes passed, and the boy saw the Dragon King of the Eastern Sea float to the surface of the ocean, along with his defeated army of shrimp soldiers and crab generals, who were crying for mercy after having been nearly boiled to death in that bubbling, red-hot sea. "Turn back the tide and return the land!" the boy commanded the Dragon King. "Call back the winds and quiet the waves, or I will keep boiling you! Would you have me boil you to death, Dragon King?"

'The Dragon King had no choice but to obey. He quieted the wind and quelled the waves, and in an instant the storms ceased, the typhoons were put to rest, the sun emerged and the sea was tranquil. The waters receded, the land reappeared, and green rice seedlings sprouted all over the Village of the Marsh.

Seeing this, the villagers gathered onshore began to applaud and cheer. The Sea Child removed the cauldron and extinguished the fire beneath it. As soon as the fire had been extinguished, however, the Dragon King made a surprise comeback. He called up a wave that swept the cauldron back into the sea, where it disappeared for ever. In an instant, the village was transformed once more into an endless stretch of waves and typhoon-swept waters.

'The Sea Child was furious. What was he to do? He stamped his enormous feet in anger and the entire village, from the mountains to the sea, began to shake. The impact of the quake caused the gold buried beneath the surface to go flying into the air. At the sight of all the gold, the villagers rushed forward to snatch up the treasure, but they soon discovered, to their amazement, that as the gold nuggets fell to the ground, they turned into stone. As the stones fell from the sky, they formed a wall around the entire village to protect the land from the ocean tides. From that day forward, the villagers realised that all of the gold that had been buried underground had turned to stone, so they stopped being so greedy. They stopped chasing after fortunes and turned to fishing instead. Now that there was a wall to protect the village from the sea, they were able to lead a peaceful life. They settled down and raised families, and the village grew larger and more prosperous. From that day forward, the village was renamed Village of Stone . . .'

This was the story that the old stationmaster told me that afternoon in the village bus station. He talked for a very long time, until the sun had disappeared behind the hills and I heard my grandmother's voice in the distance, shouting for me to come home:

'Little Dog . . . Little Dog! Get yourself home to eat . . . !'

14

After my grandfather died, my grandmother seemed to grow much sunnier, her mournful sighs less frequent. It was as if his death had freed her from the penance she had been living under since she first arrived in the Village of Stone as a child bride. His death was her liberation. I look back upon those years as my grandmother's happiest times. On calm, sunny days she would move her cane chair outside to bask in the sun and watch the passers-by. She had no hopes, no cares. She seemed to be counting out the days one by one, reckoning up the scant remains of her time on earth. She even stopped going to the well for water. Every few days, Boy Waiting's mother brought us a bucket of fresh water. Occasionally, if she had cooked something particularly delicious, she would bring over an extra bowl. My grandmother and I were like a couple of beggars, one young and one old. All we asked of each new day was a full belly and a warm place to sleep. Sometimes the life of a beggar is a care-free one.

My grandmother particularly enjoyed the days in early October, when the typhoons had passed. Bamboo poles appeared all over the village, hung with clothes and bedding that had been mouldering all summer long. The village women got out their laundry sticks and set to beating the moisture out of their heavy quilts. The sound of laundry sticks echoed down the alley-ways, carried on waves of golden sunlight. The whole village resounded with it. Only when the quilts had been battered to the soft, spongy consistency of a steamed bun did the women relent. My grandmother sat outside in her cane chair and immersed herself in her favourite hobby: making decorative birds from the discarded bones of fish. My grandmother could fashion a bird in flight from nothing more than a single fish skeleton. The birds were a traditional handicraft of the Village of Stone, but only a few women still knew how to make them. Most of the women in the village were too busy supplementing their incomes by shelling shrimp for the seafood cold processing plant. They had neither the time nor the patience to fiddle around with piles of discarded fishbones. As someone who had married into the Village of Stone, my grandmother had done her best to master the traditional handicrafts of the village women. When it came to making these fishbone birds, she had surpassed her teachers. She never used glue or string, but relied instead on the natural angles and curvatures of the skeletons to piece and weave the bones together. Each bird was made from one complete fish skeleton. She even used the fish eyeballs, so that her creations appeared unusually lifelike. Sometimes she hollowed out the white egg-sacs of cuttlefish and fashioned them into fleets of tiny fishing boats.

My grandmother collected all sorts of fish skeletons: broad flat yellow croaker, long delicate hairtail, thick sturdy eel and the curved outer shells of shrimp. In her calloused hands, their spiny bones became soft and pliable and were transformed into tiny phoenixes, mandarin ducks, white cranes, eagles and skylarks that she lined up on the hearth. Soon our hearth was filled with little birds. Village children began flocking to our house to see them, oohing and aahing over my grandmother's creations. Now and then, the children would steal one of the birds – an eagle, perhaps, or a crane. When my grandmother discovered this, she decided that she might as well go ahead and give all the children gifts. She presented them with tiny fishing boats, which the children liked to set afloat in basins of water. All in all, my grandmother seemed very content.

It seemed that my grandmother's life had reduced itself to three main concerns: eating meals, making fishbone birds and reciting sutras. My grandmother always recited her sutras in the kitchen, before the white porcelain statue of Guanyin that graced our hearth. After she had finished her recitation for the day, she would light a stick of incense, bow and place the burning stick in her old, battered incense burner. The burner was filled with ashes that looked as if they had not been emptied in centuries. As soon as she had lit the incense and the house was filled with the fragrant smoke, my grandmother would go back outside to sit in the sunshine in her cane chair and work on her fishbone birds.

It amazed me that my grandmother, who was so illiterate that she could not even write her own name, could manage to memorise entire volumes of sutras perfectly. She could recite them by heart, word for word and line by line, jabbing at each ideograph with her blue-veined fingers for emphasis. 'Form is emptiness, emptiness is form . . .' she would recite, pointing out the ideographs rendered in brush calligraphy, pages of words she couldn't possibly have recognised. Line by line, page by page she 'read', moistening her fingers with saliva to turn the pages, until she had finished the entire book of sutras. Sometimes she asked Boy Waiting's mother to help her with a passage, often at the beginning of a new page. Hearing the first word of it was usually enough to jog my grandmother's memory. From there, she could recite the rest of the passage by heart, even with the book closed. Sometimes she would lose her place, or find that she had been reciting the wrong part, but she always managed to put herself right. She could probably have recited the sutras backwards if she had had to.

I had never understood the meaning of those tongue-twisting sutras. If there were any meaning in them, I suspect that only Guanyin herself understood it. I don't think my grandmother had a much better grasp on the mysterious workings of heaven than I did, but she never asked anyone what the sutras meant. She seemed to 'feel that faith was sufficient, and that if she persisted in her recitations of the sutras, eventually they would reveal their meaning to her. I was inclined to doubt this.

My grandmother had paid two yuan for her book of sutras,

written top to bottom in brush calligraphy on rough bamboo parchment. The old man who wrote letters for the villagers at the post office had copied it out for her. It was probably the first time he had ever been asked to copy a whole volume of Buddhist sutras. Most of the villagers only needed brief letters written. He must have put a lot of time and effort into copying that thick book of sutras, for the language was difficult and there could be no mistakes. Two yuan was no small sum in those days, but as his usual charge was thirty cents for a one-page letter or fifty cents for a two-page letter, two yuan for an entire book of sutras meant that he must have given my grandmother a considerable discount.

One day two men from outside the village came to our house looking for my grandmother. They said that they were interested in buying some of the birds she made from fish skeletons. I thought this was interesting, because it was the first time I had ever heard of anyone willing to pay money for the things. It turned out that the two men were rather high-ranking cadres from the provincial headquarters. They wandered around our kitchen taking photographs of my grandmother's bird sculptures, which were lined up on the hearth and along the window sills. When they had finished, they watched my grandmother nimbly working on one of her creations. They seemed quite fascinated, clucking their tongues and shaking their heads in admiration. Because my grandmother was sitting outside in her cane chair the entire time, she soon attracted a crowd of curious onlookers. Passers-by and neighbours ran over to see what all the fuss was about, and stood alongside the visiting cadres watching my grandmother's 'performance'. In such a small village, this was big news indeed. But my grandmother didn't feel that her silly little trifles were worthy of selling. She told the cadres to keep their cash and suggested that, in exchange for the bird sculptures, they just give us enough rice, flour and oil to get us through the winter. The visiting cadres did exactly as she asked, delivering enough food for that winter and the next. Then they packed the sturdy little sculptures into a wooden box covered with red silk and carted them away.

The village buzzed with talk of the incident. The fishermen's wives still considered my grandmother a bit of an oddball. They had spent their whole lives eating fish, mind you, but they certainly couldn't be bothered fiddling around with any discarded bones, shells, eyeballs and what have you. Although they had to give my grandmother credit for being persistent. Not only had the old girl had the patience to learn one of their traditional handicrafts, she had even managed to sell people her batty idea and trade in those little fishbone birds for stores of flour and rice. My grandmother was a strange old bird, they thought, but she was not one to be underestimated.

My grandmother and I paid no heed to what the villagers said behind our backs. We sat back and watched the villagers lugging provisions into our house, until they had filled two large vats with rice flour and green bean flour. Sometimes the villagers would even bring us water from the well to fill our cistern. Needless to say, my grandmother and I were thrilled by this turn of events.

In the years that followed my grandfather's death, my grandmother finally achieved some recognition in the village. She became even more of a village hero when high-ranking provincial officials presented her with a red-bordered plaque which proclaimed, in fancy gold lettering: 'Highest commendations to Comrade Liang Yuxiu, People's Artist.'

Comrade Liang Yuxiu. By this time, I had already been at school for years and could read the name with ease. But the name itself came as a complete shock to me, for I had never seen or heard it before. Comrade Liang Yuxiu was none other than my grandmother.

15

The eel has become a permanent fixture in our lives.

If you were to open our refrigerator, you would find it filled from top to bottom with portions of dismembered eel. The head resides on the top shelf, the upper half of the body on the second, the belly on the third, and the tail on the fourth and bottom shelf. Even after soaking for days, the head and tail were still so rigid that we had trouble stuffing them into the refrigerator. The eel now occupies most of our available refrigerator space, but the parts are wedged in so tightly that we can't be bothered to take them out again. Solidifying in the cold refrigerated air on their respective shelves, they present a truly revolting sight. Although we were careful to seal each component part in plastic wrap, the odour of eel has seeped through the confines of the refrigerator and is slowly permeating our flat. The kitchen, bathroom, bedroom/living room, even the sheets on our bed are now contaminated by the smell. The omnipresent stench of fish expands, as if by osmosis, to fill every corner of our darkened flat.

At first, Red hoped that we would finish eating the eel as quickly as possible. The sooner it was annihilated, he reckoned, the better. He even took this principle one step further, waiting until I had left for work to toss large chunks of eel into the rubbish bin. Unfortunately for him, I happened to return home from work one day and notice the eel's enormous head poking out of the bin, its glassy eyes staring vacantly into the darkness of our kitchen. How could anyone throw out a perfectly good eel head? It seemed almost a crime. I fished the head out of the bin, rinsed it off and set it on the table to dry.

But soon something happened that caused Red to stop regarding the eel in our refrigerator as his personal enemy. One afternoon we decided to go out for a walk. We had just eaten a large lunch of rice and boiled eel and, still burping from our meal, we went to get some air.

As we passed a nearby Japanese restaurant, the two kimono-clad women standing at the entrance bowed to us respectfully. Red squinted in passing at the expensive menu displayed outside the door. It featured glossy colour photos and prices of the various Japanese dishes on offer:

Sashimi boat	280 yuan
Eel on rice	90 yuan
Grilled eel	120 yuan
Grilled salmon	100 yuan
Grilled sardines	80 yuan
Eel 'maki' roll	40 yuan

Our eyes were immediately drawn to the eel dishes and their corresponding prices. I did a quick calculation in my head. At those prices, five portions of grilled eel or six point six portions of eel on rice would consume my entire monthly salary. We lingered for a moment, looking at the prices, and then attempted to walk past the kimono-clad hostesses as nonchalantly as we could.

The moment we had passed the restaurant, Red turned to me and vowed, 'I promise never to throw away any of our eel again.'

'Good,' I said.

Red was struck with another brilliant idea. 'Hey, why don't we sell our eel to the restaurant?'

It took walking past that Japanese restaurant, a place where neither of us could ever afford to eat, to make Red realise that our eel was an extremely valuable commodity.

I shook my head. Now that the eel was in my life, there was no way I was going to relinquish it.

★   ★   ★

Chomping on slices of banana-flavoured chewing gum in an effort to freshen our breath, Red and I walked back to our building. As we entered the hallway, we noticed a middle-aged woman at the far end of the corridor. She was standing in front of our flat.

'Looking for something?' Red asked rather rudely, as he pulled his keys from his pocket and began to unlock the door.

The woman started, and turned abruptly. She had obviously been so immersed in her spying activities that she hadn't noticed us standing right beside her. She must have assumed that we were inside. Chastened, she hastened to explain her presence.

'It's like this . . . I live next door with my daughter, who works for a perfume company. She's a perfumier, which means she researches formulas and ingredients for perfumes. You wouldn't believe it if I told you, but our flat is filled with books on perfume making, shelves of books, and hundreds of bottles of perfume oils and essences. Every one of them has a different scent, you know. But lately she's been having a hard time working because, well, I don't know quite how to put this, but . . . there seems to be a very strong fishy smell coming from your flat. Maybe it's a piece of rotting fish stuck in the pipes or something. Anyway, the smell is filling our flat and it's interfering with my daughter's work. She can't smell the perfume oils she's working with, and when she brings the formulas into her office, all of them smell of fish. Why, just the other day her boss criticised her for being unprofessional. The poor girl came home almost in tears. She was too embarrassed to come over and talk to you about it herself, so I volunteered to come over instead. Now, I know we're all busy and have our own problems to worry about, but I wonder if you might take a peek around the flat and try to find out what's causing the smell. If you don't have the time, I'd be willing to clean your kitchen for you, tidy things up a bit, you know. Goodness knows I could use the exercise . . .'

Perfume formulas? Perfumiers? There were actually people who made perfume formulas for a living? And one of them was living right here, on the ground floor of this building? I began to see our building in a different light. As the woman prattled on, I glanced around the crowded hall filled with old, dusty bicycles and abandoned furniture, and wondered whether perhaps there was more to this place than met the eye. It seemed that we had underestimated this building, just as we had obviously underestimated the possibility of our eel becoming a public menace. The whole time we had been living in this building, we had considered ourselves the persecuted. Now we had become the persecutors.

16

I remember that the year I turned fifteen, the heavens deluged the village with winter rain, an uncomfortably sticky rain that far overstayed its welcome. It rained for so long that the cobblestone streets, always damp to begin with, were transformed into pools of water swirling with the dead fish and shrimp that had fallen into the cracks between the cobbles during the autumn catch. Just before the twelfth moon, the rains relented and the sun reappeared at last. My grandmother carried her old cane chair outdoors so that she could bask in the rare sunshine. The sun was still bright when I went outside that afternoon and noticed that she was sitting motionless in her chair. Her head had fallen to one side, but her hands were still draped over the armrests. My grandmother had passed away so peacefully that at first, I couldn't bring myself to believe that she was really dead.

At that moment, with the sun slanting down upon her black clothes and white chignon, from which a few stray wisps of hair had escaped, she simply looked as if she were asleep.

My grandmother had always kept her incense burner on the window sill. I had never used it myself, because such offerings to the gods held no meaning for me. But after my grandmother died, the house seemed so empty, so noticeably devoid of the rising curls of bluish smoke that had once wafted through our kitchen that it was as if the incense burner had died along with my grandmother. The day after her death, I took one of the remaining sticks of incense from the box and lit it. It was the first and only time I would make such an offering.

★　★　★

Though my grandmother had passed away, I found myself forgetting that she was gone. Each evening as I stood on the beach, watching the waves grow dark and the sun making its descent into the sea, I was stricken with a sort of temporary amnesia. I half expected my grandmother, leaning on her cane, her back bent with the effort, to come walking down the length of Pirate's Alley and down to the beach. After that, I would hear her long drawn-out cries, shrill as a whistle, calling me home: *Little Dog, get yourself home to eat!*

I had always waited for my grandmother's voice, always listened for her faraway call echoing around the mountain, before I returned home for dinner, home to that large wooden table with its solitary two bowls of gruel and bottle of shrimp paste. But now there was nothing awaiting me there: no voice calling, no dinner laid. There was nothing awaiting me, and nothing to wait for.

I began to look upon my grandmother's death as a good thing. After all, she had died of old age. It was a peaceful death, the kind of death everyone hopes for. And her passing had brought her the kind of good fortune she had never known while she was alive. Although she was not a native of the Village of Stone and had come into it only by marriage, she would never again find herself shunted aside by the villagers. She now had her very own patch of earth, a place on the mountain beside the brackish sea, where she could rest in eternal slumber. She had finally become a part of the Village of Stone. Her suffering had ceased, and happiness was hers at last.

That winter seemed to pass very quickly. Solar terms followed one upon another – first the Lesser Snow, then the Greater Snow (although, as usual, there was no snow in the Village of Stone) and then, before I knew it, the New Year was at hand. For the fishermen and their wives, New Year meant a period of safety, a respite from fishing. For the village children it meant the delicious anticipation of New Year treats and new holiday clothes. It was always a busy time in the village. The lights in the houses went on in the small hours of the morning and were not extinguished until late at night, and the kitchens were a bustle of activity all day long. In the midst of all this, I suddenly found myself alone, a single teenager on the verge of adulthood with no parents, grandparents, siblings, cousins, aunts or uncles. I was alone in the world.

So I carried on alone. The strange thing is that I never once lost hope. Like a tiny sand crab hiding in the cracks between the rocks along the shoreline, I simply kept to myself and kept growing up.

17

'Do you know the Marianas Trench?' I ask Red. I am lying on our mattress on the floor and staring up at the ceiling.

'The Marianas what?' Red scratches his head.

'The Marianas Trench. It's the deepest ocean trench in the world.'

I feel my train of thought projecting upwards, bursting through the ceiling and the twenty-five storeys overhead, sailing off into the infinite distance.

'The Marianas Trench has a depth of eleven thousand and thirty-four metres.'

'Eleven thousand and thirty-four metres . . .' Red mumbles, as if repeating the figure will somehow make it less of an abstraction.

I doubt whether it would be possible to live in a twenty-five storey high-rise, particularly one as crowded and hideously ugly as ours, and still retain the imagination required to grasp the idea of the Marianas Trench.

'Where is the Marianas Trench?' Red asks.

'In the South Pacific.'

Red gazes blankly out the window. Our forty-five minutes of early morning sunlight have already packed up and departed, leaving the balcony in darkness.

'In the deepest parts of the ocean, even the fish are flat. It's because of the water pressure . . .' I add in an undertone.

I am talking to myself now. I know that there are some things that, no matter how infinitely deep they are buried, will always come floating back to the surface.

★   ★   ★

Distant memory is the Marianas Trench of the soul.

This time it is my teacher, Mr Mou, who floats up from the depths of my Marianas Trench, from the waters of my Village of Stone.

My memories of him run too deep, so deep that there isn't enough oxygen to sustain them. This lack of oxygen has caused his memory to pale and thin, leaving only disconnected shards and muddied images. But my memory of Mr Mou is like the sea of the Village of Stone. No matter how muddied, an ocean is still an ocean, tempestuous and frightening in its intensity.

Mr Mou is yet another dark undercurrent in my memory. Even after all these years, memories of him continue to well up into my present consciousness.

18

The year I turned fifteen, my body began to emerge from its childhood cave. As the sun shone down upon me, I remained oblivious to the fact that my body was growing. I grew taller, grew out of the fearful child I once was and into a young woman. My plaited hair, once so thin and frazzled, grew as thick and dark as the inky seaweed growing in the kelp beds along the shore. It spilled over my shoulders and down my back. It was as if I had become an adult almost overnight. With the help of Boy Waiting's parents, I enrolled at the only secondary school in the Village of Stone.

I never knew where Mr Mou, my chemistry teacher, came from. Had he been born in the Village of Stone? Was he already living in the village at the time I was born? Or was he an outsider like my grandmother, someone who had moved here from an inland village far away from the sea?

When I think back about Mr Mou after all these years, I realise that he had certain qualities that marked him out as different from the other villagers. He was gentle and kind, incapable of cruelty or violence. Perhaps that was the reason I was so immediately drawn to him.

It started during my second year at the school. I remember that it was nearing the end of summer, and that the typhoons were still raging. They always came from the east, gaining strength as they swept over the East China Sea, until at last they spiralled from the skies and touched down in the Village of Stone. The typhoons inundated the village, tossed it to and fro as if it were but a small wooden bucket bobbing on the surface of an endless sea.

I had already noticed how long and pale Mr Mou's hands were, and how he always seemed to be alone. He was alone when he emerged from his office, alone when he paced around the schoolyard, alone when he walked down the street outside the schoolhouse. He was very fair, his face almost as pale and delicate as his long, slender hands. He wore his hair rather long, the locks tumbling over his forehead. This made him look very different from the other teachers at our school.

In my eyes, he was truly an exception to the rule. Instead of marking our homework notebooks in red pen like the other teachers in our little village school, Mr Mou used a stone stamp dipped in red ink. He had three different stamps that he had carved by hand himself; each was the shape of an animal. A lion stamp symbolised 'excellent' marks, a tiger stamp was 'good' and a rabbit stamp meant 'poor'. At first, all the stamps in my home-work notebook were tigers, indicating that my chemistry marks were about average. As my marks in inorganic chemistry grad-ually improved, the tigers changed to lions and I managed to earn five lions in the course of the term. I had grown to like chemistry. Or, I suppose you could say, I had grown to like my chemistry teacher.

One afternoon, I was leaning on my desk in chemistry class listening to my classmates trying to memorise the periodic table of elements for a forthcoming test: *Hydrogen, Helium, Lithium, Beryllium, Boron, Carbon, Nitrogen, Oxygen, Fluorine, Neon, Sodium, Magnesium, Aluminium* . . . I was too tired to study. The cicadas were buzzing outside the window and there was the feeling in the air that a round of storms was brewing. It was hot and humid, and rain seemed imminent. As the time for class drew nearer, the clamour in the classroom intensified. The students, struggling to memorise the periodic table, turned up the volume and frequency of their recitations. The collective chant grew louder, the frequencies intensified and the hiss of voices began to sound like something being stir-fried.

Though the other students were nervous about the test, I was not at all anxious. I wasn't afraid of being punished if I received a poor mark. After all, what could my teachers do to me? How could they inflict a punishment worse than what I had already endured? The stifling afternoon heat was making me drowsy, and it seemed like the most natural thing in the world to lay my head on my desk and rest. The bell rang, signalling the start of class, and Mr Mou entered the classroom carrying a test tube and a Bunsen burner. He set the test tube gently on the burner, and the classroom full of students quieted down. Dragging my head from the desk, I propped it up with my elbows and made a token effort to keep my eyes riveted to the front of the classroom, so that I would appear to be listening to the lecture rather than dozing. So intently did I focus on looking straight ahead and keeping my eyes wide open that, from Mr Mou's vantage point, it must have looked as if I were glaring at him through the entire class.

Some time afterwards, I ran into Mr Mou as he was wheeling his decrepit bicycle out of the schoolyard. I remember that he was wearing an orange shirt that day, and seemed to be in rather low spirits. As I passed him at the gate, we happened to glance at each other. He stopped to mention that he had seen an angry young woman glaring up at him one day during chemistry class. No matter how hard he had tried, he told me, he could not manage to avoid her gaze.

'Oh, that . . .' I made an effort to explain. 'I was just feeling tired.'

'But I've noticed that you have the same expression even when you aren't tired.'

'Oh yeah?' I answered apathetically.

Mr Mou continued pushing his bicycle and made no reply. As we reached the wrought-iron front gate of the schoolyard, he suddenly spoke.

The eyes he had seen, he told me, were not the eyes of a fifteen-year-old girl. They were the eyes of a wild animal, something wary and constantly on its guard, a creature that could never be tamed.

That was more or less what I had become at the age of fifteen: a wild animal with an inborn hatred of the world.

Mr Mou wanted to know what had made me that way, what had happened to turn me into the despondent, wild-eyed creature he saw in his classes.

That was how our story began. We were only eight years apart. Mr Mou was rather young, for a teacher.

One evening, Mr Mou and I climbed to the top of the mountain behind the Village of Stone. We stood in the graveyard beneath the full moon hanging over the roiling sea, looking down at the expanse of inky darkness below. On the slope of the mountain, the grass growing over the graves swayed softly in the breeze, and fireflies flitted between the headstones. Among all those graves, where generation upon generation of villagers lay buried, were my grandfather and grandmother.

There, beneath the moonlight, I reached for Mr Mou's hand, although I wasn't at all afraid of ghosts. I wasn't afraid of anything.

I told him that I didn't like family. Family was a thing I could never love again.

This seemed to shock him. 'Why wouldn't you love your family?'

'No particular reason,' I answered. 'It's just that family is meaningless.'

'How can family be meaningless?' He was genuinely puzzled now.

'Because family can't make a person happy. Family doesn't mean a thing.'

It was a roundabout answer. I didn't dare tell Mr Mou about my grandparents, or about the things that had happened to me when I was seven.

Mr Mou gazed at me for a very long time but said nothing. After a while, we both raised our heads to look at the moon, that lonely and desolate sphere hanging frozen in the black sky. At that moment, the moon seemed every bit as cold as my world.

'I know about your parents,' Mr Mou finally said. 'I know that you lost them both. That must be very painful for you.'

Although I was a bit surprised to hear Mr Mou admit this, I also had the feeling that he had known about my parents, and about me, all along. I never asked what else he knew about me, or where he had heard it. I was just glad to know that he had noticed.

Below us, I could hear seagulls, a whole flock of them, crying out one after another. I felt the salt breeze on my forehead.

Mr Mou spoke again, softly this time. 'You always look so frightened.'

Did I? I wasn't sure what made him think so, because there was nothing that could frighten me, at least not any more. Death, tombstones, ghosts . . . what was so frightening about those? What could be more frightening than that pit in the earth I had known when I was seven years old?

Thinking about this, I suddenly started to laugh. In all my fifteen years, it was the first time I could ever remember laughing.

Mr Mou kept his eyes riveted on my face until my newfound laughter faded, almost as quickly as it had come.

'So you *can* laugh, after all,' Mr Mou said at last. 'You have a beautiful smile.' He gazed into my eyes, from which the laughter had died, as if they concealed an ocean of secrets.

I wanted to say something, but I could think of nothing to say.

The air was filled with night sounds – pine needles rustling in the breeze, the cries of the seabirds, the tips of their silver wings skimming over the water, and the sound of fishermen dragging their nets across the beach. The sounds were faint and peaceful, comforting somehow.

We sat watching the moon slide west across the evening sky. We made no move to go home because neither of us wanted to leave. Leaving meant going back home alone, back to our separate lives, until the next day when we would once again find ourselves in the same classroom, the same and very public place.

'Mr Mou, I'm cold . . .'

He put his arms around me and opened his jacket so that I

could nestle inside. His chest was so warm. In that warm, tiny world I could still hear the sound of the ocean.

There under the moonlight, on the far side of the mountain of the Village of Stone, Mr Mou whispered to me, 'You're still just a child.'

I raised my head so that I could look at him. 'I'm not a child. I've been old almost since I can remember.'

Mr Mou looked at me in surprise. His eyes were like the ocean below, a reflection of moonlight on the waves. He gazed at me for such a long time, so very long that I could see the waning moon over his shoulder, making its slow descent into the western sky.

I've forgotten so many of the details. But I will always remember our first time.

His house was rather bare, the floors littered with carving tools and oddly shaped stones. I noticed that the three familiar stone stamps he used in our homework notebooks – lion, tiger and rabbit – had been tossed carelessly upon his cluttered desktop. Until that moment, I had considered those stamps somehow sacred, because they symbolised our chemistry marks and Mr Mou's authority as a teacher. In his hand, they had the power to determine whether we were outstanding lions, average tigers or simply rabbits who had failed to earn even a pass. But as I stood there before Mr Mou's untidy desk, I realised that in his hands, these stamps were nothing more than playthings.

What kind of person was this man, my teacher, I wondered.

At first, we simply stood together beside his bed. Mr Mou seemed extremely nervous, though I felt calm and composed. So calm, in fact, that I wondered how I could help him overcome his nervousness. For a long time, neither of us spoke. All I could hear was the sound of his ragged breathing.

No longer was he my teacher. He was just a man without experience. A little boy, really.

Finally, we sat down on his bed. I took his hand in mine and guided it to my chest, let it linger there, feeling the warmth and softness. Mr Mou said nothing. Silently, obediently, he followed my lead as I helped him to unbutton my blouse, reach inside and touch my skin.

From start to finish, I was the one helping him, the one guiding him. It was as if I were the teacher and he the student. He trembled like a child.

I never meant to hurt him. I didn't think that I could hurt him.

His was a single bed, cramped and narrow. Lying there, my body small and pale, I felt as pure and unsullied as a newborn child. Naturally, I told Mr Mou nothing of my secret. I wanted him to believe that mine was the body of a young girl, pure and innocent.

In the light slanting through the shutters, I could see that Mr Mou was blushing. The pale blue shutters rattled softly in the light summer breeze and bands of sunlight falling through the slats played over Mr Mou's face, making him look anxious and bewildered.

And then he was inside me.

There was no blood. No blood, no sound, nothing. Not even pain.

Afterwards, I saw whitish fluid. It was not unfamiliar.

I never meant to hurt him.

I thought I was helping him, really I did. Helping him to become a man.

It was my first sexual experience as an equal.

Afterwards, he said he wished it hadn't happened. I never had any regrets.

But I could tell he was ashamed. He sat on the edge of the bed, just staring at the shutters and watching the waning sunlight cast shadows on the bedroom wall.

We had tumbled into an abyss. An abyss in which the only warmth came from one another's bodies. In that abyss, I finally felt safe and free.

Mr Mou was blameless. I can swear to that.

But in that abyss, that world our two bodies had made, even my love would not prove to be enough to assuage Mr Mou's guilty conscience.

I discovered that I was pregnant in the middle of that term. Exams were approaching and Mr Mou had started assigning revision questions in his class. But I had already stopped attending chemistry class. Whilst the other students laboured over their equations, I waited at Mr Mou's house, watching the clock on the wall, until it was time to put on my backpack and leave to attend my other required courses. I still had Chinese, maths, political science and physical education classes to attend. I had started feeling sick during lessons. I did what I could to control the nausea, but there was no question about what was happening to my body. I was certain I was pregnant.

None of this frightened me. When I told Mr Mou the news, however, he was devastated.

We decided that I should get an abortion, but I was afraid to go to the hospital. I was fifteen years old, but I looked closer to twelve because I was so short and petite. Mr Mou told me that I would have to try to look older, at least twenty. To this end, he bought me a loose blouse, a tight black skirt and a pair of high heels. With lipstick, I just about passed for a young woman who had graduated from school. But Mr Mou said I still looked too young. My expression, he said, was that of a child.

We did not dare to go to the village hospital, where all the doctors would know us. Instead, Mr Mou bought a bus ticket at the station and made a trip to another village to look at the hospital there. Perhaps because Mr Mou was a teacher, a well-respected and educated man, the old stationmaster did not ask him where he was going or why. The hospital was a long bus ride away through tunnels and over mountains. When Mr Mou returned, he assured me that nobody would know us there. The hospital had an obstetrics and gynaecology department that performed abortions. I could even register under a false name, he said.

We decided to leave that Saturday at noon. On Saturday morning, I donned my regular clothes, placed my disguise in a bag and went to school as usual. Although I felt terribly uneasy, I somehow managed to get through the morning's classes without incident. Mr Mou was not teaching that morning. He had gone to borrow some money for the abortion, but we had arranged to meet after school, at the school gate.

When the bell rang at noon, signalling the end of classes, I trailed after the crowd of students rushing out of the school gate. The sun was shining brightly, high in the sky. I craned my neck, looking for Mr Mou, but he was nowhere to be found. I waited and waited, as the sun went from being a ball of light to some blood-red thing, a creature with a wide crimson mouth and tongue of flame. It seemed as if all the world were as red as fresh-spilled blood. I stood at the gate of the schoolyard unblinking, staring at the sun, and began to feel faint. I could see the shape of the child in my belly . . . he was lovely . . . but his four limbs were covered in blood. I felt that I had seen that blood before, perhaps on the floor of a rowing boat, somewhere in the waters off the coast of the Village of Stone. It was the fresh-spilled blood of death. But it was not the blood of a child, no . . . it was the blood of a mother giving birth. Yes, I could see things more clearly now. My child was blameless. He didn't deserve to die. I couldn't let a part of myself die. I couldn't bear to kill something that I loved.

My mother had died, Boy at Last had died, my grandmother and grandfather had died. I did not want to be responsible for bringing any more death into this world. I did not want my baby to die.

Then I saw Mr Mou standing with his backpack by a hardware stall down the road. I saw him frowning in the sunlight. He seemed more helpless than me. As he walked towards me, I shook my head and told him, 'No. I don't want to go.'

We did not keep our appointment at the hospital that day.

After midterm exams were over, things grew more difficult for Mr Mou. My bouts of nausea were more serious and I stopped attending class. Not just chemistry class this time, but all of my classes. At school, I had come to be considered something of a delinquent so nobody yet guessed my secret. But it was only a matter of time.

Mr Mou told me that if I didn't have an abortion soon, we would both have to leave the school. This wasn't just about me, he said. It affected him too.

I looked Mr Mou in the eye and told him that the school could go to hell as far as I was concerned.

For a long time, neither of us was willing to compromise. But in the end, I was the one who capitulated.

We decided that we would follow our original plan, but this time Mr Mou was adamant that we should meet at the hardware stall, to avoid being noticed. The sheets of metal, hammers and nails displayed on the hardware stall gleamed in the sunlight. The young proprietor stared at us openly, as if he knew our secret, so we hurried away as quickly as possible to avoid his accusing gaze. I had brought my 'adult clothes' along in a bag so that I could change into them later. When we arrived at the bus station, the place was deserted. Though we had been told that a bus departed each day at noon for the neighbouring villages, there was no sign of it anywhere. Mr Mou went into the station office to talk to the old stationmaster, who informed him that the bus had broken down and would be in repairs all afternoon. Mr Mou was alarmed by this news, although he was careful not to say as much to the stationmaster. The station-master must have sensed something, however, for he asked Mr Mou if his trip to the neighbouring village was urgent. 'If it is,' the stationmaster offered, 'I can help you hitch a ride on a tractor. There's a tractor over at the cold processing plant that should be leaving the village any minute now.'

When the old stationmaster emerged from the office, he noticed me standing in a corner by the front gate. He said nothing, just glanced at me quickly and limped out of the gate and over to the cold processing plant to ask about the tractor.

As I've always said, the stationmaster was a kind man.

The tractor took us down the coast and through the long mountain tunnels. We travelled far away from the village, until the sea was no longer visible and the salt breezes had dissipated. When we arrived at the hospital, Mr Mou offered to help me register for the operation. If I liked, he said, I could use an assumed name so that nobody would know who I was. 'Why would I use an assumed name?' I asked him. 'Nobody knows my real name, anyway. They've always called me Little Dog. I'll just use my real name.'

Mr Mou did not press the matter further. I went to the obstetrics and gynaecology department and registered myself under my real name, Coral Jiang.

I was led into a cramped, rather dirty little operating theatre. As I lay, spread-eagled and naked from the waist down, upon the cold, narrow table, I saw the female doctor take up a sharp instrument. From the region between my legs, I heard the sound of cutting, vacuuming, the clang of metal instruments, and then something else. It was the sound of my own flesh, my baby, being tossed into a white surgical pan.

When I had lowered my legs and was sitting, pale and exhausted, on the edge of the surgery table, I saw the doctor holding a surgery pan filled with something that looked like a chunk of raw meat. He – or she? – was hardly formed yet, nothing more than an indistinct lump of flesh.

In a voice completely devoid of emotion, the doctor told me, 'That's it. We cut out half, and had to vacuum out the other half.'

The doctor's voice was exactly like the surgical instruments she had used. Cold and sharp.

I was exhausted, my hair damp with sweat. But I had not cried once.

I dressed slowly, putting on my clothes one piece at a time. The oversized shirt, the stretchy black skirt, the pair of white high heels . . . the doctor gazed at my sweat-stained face for several moments before she finally asked, 'How old are you, really?'

I made no reply.

I turned my back to her and began to leave. As I was walking towards the door, she spoke again, this time very slowly. 'It's possible that you may not be able to have children after this . . .'

I stumbled out of the surgery, my head reeling, and made my way towards Mr Mou, who had been waiting for me outside the door. In his panic-stricken eyes, I saw my shame reflected, a flame rising around me from all sides. It was a shame I recognised, a shame I had come to know well. Somehow I had expected that growing up was the one thing that would cure me of that shame. Apparently I was wrong.

After leaving the hospital, we hitched a ride back to the village on another tractor. My face was drawn and pale, my hair askew, one hand resting limply in Mr Mou's grip. I had little energy for the journey back home. Mr Mou clutched my hand tightly, as if he were afraid that if he loosened his grasp in the slightest, he would lose me entirely. The ride was a bumpy one; each time the tractor shuddered, so did we. Neither of us spoke during the ride. As the horizon of the ocean came into view and we drew nearer to the Village of Stone, I knew that we were both feeling the same grief, the same emptiness. I was so sad that I thought I would burst into tears at any moment.

But I didn't cry that day.

My body felt hollow. My baby was gone. I had seen him fly up and away, into an ocean of sunlight overhead. He had the strangest shape. At first he was lovely, but as my vision grew clearer, I saw that my baby's eyes, the eyes of my dead child, were not eyes at all but huge dark caverns, enormous black holes that looked as if they might swallow the world at any moment. His skin was so pale, so translucent, like an egg stripped of its shell. He floated through the air, spotless and pure, every bit of him an angel. But when I looked at his fingers and toes, I realised that there was something wrong with my baby. His hands and feet were webbed, like a newly hatched duckling that had just broken its way out of its shell. His fingers and toes were still connected, as if waiting for the knife that would cut into them, make them separate at last. His white belly gave him the appearance of a float attached to a fishing line, or a drowning child. My baby was turning, changing shape before my eyes. One moment, he was Boy at Last, drowning in the seaweed beds; the next, he was me at the age of seven, being held captive in a pit underground, surrounded by darkness and violence. Then he was shrinking, smaller and smaller, trans-forming himself into a little brown bottle that took me a moment to recognise. I realised it was the bottle of DDV that my grandfather had swallowed. My baby had become a terri-fying thing, an object of fear and loathing. No longer was he something lovely, flying through the air. He had become a blot upon the sun, a black birthmark, a dark cloud from which sunlight could only seep around the edge, make its way around his massive bulk.

Mr Mou and I returned to the village and to school, where we behaved as if nothing had happened. But while we had been away at the hospital, something had changed. Someone had managed to find out our secret and had, in turn, informed everyone else at school. Before long, the entire village knew, and had formed a hostile and united front against us. There was no way I could go on living in the village after this, not as a woman of ill repute. Every detail of my difficult lot in life had become the stuff of village gossip, fodder for the neighbours' wagging tongues. One day I was told that the headmaster wanted to speak to me. I was led to his office. I could not help but notice that the loudspeaker in the school courtyard was right outside the office window. I managed to tear my eyes away from the loudspeaker long enough to focus on the principal, who was saying:

'Coral Jiang, we simply cannot allow a student such as your-self to continue at this school.'

As I walked out of the principal's office, I knew that the loudspeaker would soon be broadcasting the news of my expulsion.

At the time, I thought that I must be exactly what people said I was: a black stain on the reputation of the Village of Stone.

But what was the sea, if not a wide black stain on this earth?

I made no attempt to defend myself, or to go on living in the Village of Stone. I was truly an orphan now, in every sense of the word.

That year, I left the Village of Stone for ever.

I had been living in Beijing for several years when I received a letter from Mr Mou. It had somehow been passed between the many different addresses I had inhabited in those early years, and had found its way into my hands. The letter was as logical and orderly as one of Mr Mou's chemical equations.

Dearest Coral,

Hello. I hope you don't find it strange that I am writing to you so suddenly, after all these years. I wonder whether you still recognise my handwriting. You must always have known that I would write to you some day.

When I think about love, I realise that in my life, I have known two rays of light: yours, and the one that illuminates my life today.

Love, you see, is like a ray of light. It cannot bend, nor can it travel round corners. All it can do is reflect and refract until it loses its radiance. I think that now perhaps the time has come for our light, that ray that has persisted between us for so long, to fade away.

Rather than say that love is like a ray of light, perhaps it would be better to liken it to an organic life form, a living organism. The more elements contained within an organic life form, the more quickly it decomposes, the more powerful the scent it emits. Yours is a scent that has lingered with me all these years, even to this very day.

The other light in my life these days is changeless and eternal, more like an inorganic form of life. If buried, it will never break down into the soil, nor will it turn to coal. Yes, I am married now, Coral, and I am happy.

I am still teaching at the Village of Stone middle school, and have been promoted to form master, a job which keeps me quite busy.

The jasmine trees are in full bloom, and the entire village is being mobilised for this year's typhoon prevention activities. The typhoons will soon be upon us.

I wish you every happiness, Coral. May you have a wonderful life and a beautiful future.

Sincerely yours,
Mr Mou
30 June, 3.00 p.m.

I read Mr Mou's unexpected letter over again and again. I must have read it a dozen times. At first I wanted to write back to him, to tell him that I still loved him, even after all these years. Suddenly, his love seemed to me like something that had happened only yesterday, something that I had only just lost. But when I read the letter again, I realised that it was not the sort of message that required an answer. There was not a single sentence about me. He had not even bothered to ask me about my life or about how I was faring. It was as if our connection had already been severed. The letter was nothing more than Mr Mou's final farewell, his official declaration of goodbye.

I put the letter away and decided that I would never read it again.

That is all there is to the story of Mr Mou, the man I loved, and the baby I never had. I have buried them at the bottom of my Marianas Trench. Now and then, I might hear the sound of an infant wailing, a voice rising from the darkness of the trench, but these are soon swallowed up in the black vortex, drowned in the abyss of my memory.

Red, you know nothing of this Marianas Trench. You have not yet penetrated its depths, nor have you any clue to the stories buried eleven thousand and thirty-four metres below its surface.

19

I wake at eight o'clock, just in time to catch the sunlight, but the weather refuses to cooperate. The sky outside remains overcast, as dark and gloomy as my mood. Red is not lying beside me. I hear water running in the bathroom and Red singing to himself in the shower. He is humming a tune by the Taiwanese pop singer Zhao Chuan: *I'm just a little bird who wants to fly / but I never seem to get too high / I'm still searching for a bit of sky* . . . I glance at the clock. Why is my little bird up so early today?

Then I remember: it is the Frisbee tournament today.

A while later, Red comes back into the bedroom, a towel slung around his neck. Still damp from his shower, he rummages through the wardrobe for a pair of blue shorts and a white T-shirt.

I sit up in bed. My body feels sluggish and heavy.

I glance over at Red, who is pulling on a pair of white sports socks. He looks so relaxed, as if he has not a care in this world. Maybe it is true that a man has to enjoy his carefree years while he can, to cling to them so that he will have something to remember after he hits thirty and finds his life complicated by other responsibilities. I can imagine exactly the way Red will look today, playing Frisbee on a field of green grass.

I hear the burglar-proof metal front door closing, and then the sound of Red's footsteps receding down the hall. I am alone in the apartment now, and my bad mood has not improved one bit. I get out of bed, throw on a flimsy negligee and go into the bathroom to give myself a chrysanthemum facial mask.

I have just smeared white paste all over my face when the doorbell rings.

Who can it be? I guess it must be Red, coming back for something he has forgotten. Without even bothering to throw anything over my negligee or wash the mask from my face, I run to the door and throw it wide open.

The man standing outside my door is a complete stranger.

My first reaction is to try to cover myself by placing my hands strategically over the more revealing portions of my skimpy negligee. But even more embarrassing than my attire is the white mask I am still wearing on my face.

The old man standing outside my door – I say old man, for he appears to be quite elderly – is looking at me intently. There is something strange about his gaze that I cannot quite put my finger on, but it makes me uncomfortable.

With the wet, sticky mask still clinging to my face, I must look like a madwoman. All I want is to put an end to this awkward moment as quickly as possible. The man must have come to the wrong house, I imagine.

I keep hoping that the old man will speak so that I can get rid of him, but he just continues to stare at me in silence.

Unable to contain my annoyance any longer, I ask him rather rudely, 'Who are you looking for?' After all, I have to say something to break the awkward silence.

Very slowly, the old man asks, 'Are you . . . Coral?'

I am too surprised to do anything but nod my head. This man is a stranger, yet he seems to know me. I find it odd that he has addressed me so casually, without even bothering to use my last name.

'So you *are* Coral Jiang?' He seems excited by the news.

Struggling to maintain my composure, I size up the man standing outside my door. He appears to be in his mid-fifties, although with his head of white hair, he could be closer to sixty. There is something about his eyes, his mouth, his manner of speaking that is oddly familiar, and yet I am sure that I have never met him before.

I am struck by a sudden premonition, a premonition so powerful that I tremble at the very thought of it. Oh god, I think, please oh please don't let it be true.

I stiffen almost unconsciously, as if bracing myself for a shock.

The old man is still standing outside. 'May I come in?' he asks politely.

We gaze at each other for a few moments. His is the face of a kind man; he seems harmless enough.

Without bothering to answer his question, I leave the front door slightly ajar and rush back into the apartment to tidy myself up. I duck my head under the tap in the bathroom and towel off the bits of mask still sticking to my skin. Without even bothering to dry my face, I throw on a change of clothes. I am agitated, filled with conflicting and powerful emotions. My heart is racing.

After a quick glance in the mirror, I make my way back to the front door, open it wide and invite the man to come in.

Now that he can see my face clearly, the old man seems somewhat shocked. His eyes remain riveted to my face.

Have I forgotten to wash something off? I wipe at my face self-consciously.

The man enters the flat rather timidly and stands in the small corridor between the kitchen and bathroom. From the corridor, he can see right into our messy bedroom. Piled upon the bed, in a tangle of sheets, are Red's pants and socks and my underwear. The old man casts a sidelong glance at the poster from *Ulysses' Gaze* that is hanging on the bedroom wall. Harvey Keitel stares right back at him.

Before I can say a word, the old man turns to me and says, very slowly and deliberately: 'I am your father.'

For a moment, the world stands still.

I stand in the cramped corridor staring at this man, this stranger who claims to be my father.

What should I say? What *can* I say?

I have nothing to say.

The only words I can manage are, 'Have a seat.'

The words are absolutely meaningless. Both of us remain standing.

Regardless of whether the man really is my father or just some crazy person, I feel that I ought at least to offer him something to drink. I go into the kitchen and pour him a glass of water, then set it on the small table in the hallway.

At this point, I have no idea what I should do next. Check his residence permit? Ask for his name? Place of birth? Age? Occupation? Ask where he has come from, or how he has come to be here? Or, assuming he really *is* my father, ask him why the hell he hasn't tried to find me sooner?

The old man does not even touch the glass of water I have poured for him.

I look down at the shirt covering my short negligee. The shirt comes down to my thighs, and my legs are bare. I realise belatedly that it must look as if I am wearing nothing at all underneath.

We stand awkwardly, face to face in the cramped hallway. Before us is a bedroom strewn with underwear, behind us is the front door. To the left and right are the kitchen and bathroom. There is nowhere for us to go. At least, nowhere that seems appropriate.

The old man speaks first. 'My name is Jiang Qinglin. I haven't been back to the Village of Stone in decades, but a few years ago I heard that you'd left the village, so I started asking around. I talked to a lot of people, spent a lot of time looking before I finally found you. I'm sorry to show up un-announced . . . I know this must seem very sudden. Do you live here alone?'

I find myself nodding before I realise, a moment too late, that I do not in fact live alone. I hasten to correct my mistake by shaking my head.

I suddenly remember what my grandfather said to me just before he died, on that rainy day:

'Little Dog, if you ever meet your father, tell him that I am an unhappy man.'

My grandfather's words were like an epitaph carved on the gravestone of a father I had never met, words attesting to my father's mistakes. I never expected to have a father turn up in my life at the late age of twenty-eight, in a city so far from my home town.

And yet now, twenty years later, I find an old man standing opposite me, telling me he is my long-lost father. How should I answer him? Should I tell him about my grandfather's last words? Maybe I should tell him how my grandfather died. Or does he already know?

Face to face with this man who claims to be my father, I have no idea what I ought to say.

He must sense this, for he suddenly straightens up and turns as if to leave. I have the feeling that he wants to say more but cannot quite find the words, or that he is hoping I will ask him something.

But I have no idea what to ask.

As he nears the front door, the old man seems to find the words he has come to say: 'Coral, I have cancer. They say it's terminal.'

I am dumbstruck.

As he opens the door, he fishes out a tattered business card.

'My telephone number is on the front.' Oblivious to the surreal nature of a father handing his daughter his business details, he passes me the card.

He is almost out of the door now. I make no effort to persuade him to stay longer. Suddenly, he seems to hesitate, as if he knows that this is the last time he will be allowed inside my apartment. As he tightens his grip on the doorknob, I notice that his hands resemble mine.

I hear him saying, 'I wasn't planning to tell you I was sick, but I found out that you were living here and I thought that you ought to know. You're my only living relative. The doctors say I haven't got long to live, two months at the most. I just wanted to meet you once. I don't expect you to take care of me. I just wanted to know how you are doing. Now that I've met you and seen that you're doing well, I can rest much easier.'

With that, he slowly opens the door and starts to leave.

'I'm sorry, Coral. I know this must have been quite a shock.'

As I watch him disappear down the corridor, I am struck by how very much he looks like an elderly Japanese man. There is something about his bearing, so polite and scrupulously poised, as if he is keeping himself in check. Then the main doors close behind him and, just like that, the old man stricken with cancer, the old man who claims to be my father, is gone.

After he has left, I wander around the flat in a daze. My mind is a complete blank.

I try to remember what the old man was wearing. He seems to have been dressed in a fairly common dark blue shirt, the sort of inexpensive shirt one can buy anywhere on the street. The fabric was of rather poor quality, his grey slacks looked as if they had never been pressed and his brown leather shoes were covered with scuff marks. His clothes were no different from the clothes worn by every other man his age. If he was my father, how could he look so identical to all of the other fathers in this city? How could the father I have imagined so often over the years look so ordinary in real life?

I begin to realise that imagination, like memory, is fallible. As time goes on, neither is to be trusted.

Though I had not imagined that my father was still alive, there have been times when I have secretly prayed that if he were still alive, he would stay away. But he has not stayed away, and now I have an image of him in my mind. Regardless of whether I want any connection with him, he has already forced a connection by telling me that he has cancer and has only two months to live. Whether this is true or not, it creates a certain pressure in my life.

I begin to feel depressed and irritable. I wish I had gone out with Red instead of hanging around the flat waiting for a madman to come knocking on my front door. If I had gone out, I would never have known about the old man with terminal cancer. I would never have known that there is an old man living in this city who claims to be my father.

It is afternoon already. I know I should eat something, but I am in no mood to eat.

I open the refrigerator and close it again. I do not feel like cooking for myself. I know that even if I do eat something, it will taste like wax.

Red comes home dripping with sweat, his body sunburned as red as a boiled lobster. He carries his Frisbee in his backpack, and his white T-shirt is covered with grass stains and bits of grass.

As he sets down his backpack and strips off his sweaty T-shirt, Red seems to notice that I am out of sorts.

'How was your day?' he asks. 'What did you do?'

'Nothing,' I lie.

'You didn't do anything at all?'

'Uh-unh.'

'What did you have for lunch?'

'I didn't have lunch.'

'You didn't eat anything at all?' Red looks at me curiously.

'Nope.'

'What's wrong? You haven't been yourself these last few days.'

'Really? How so?'

'I don't know.' Red glances up at the calendar. 'It must be that time of month. That's probably why.'

I say nothing.

'I'm dying of thirst,' Red mumbles as he picks up a glass of water from the hall table and tips it into his mouth. I notice that it is the same glass of water I poured for the man who claimed to be my father.

Red drinks the water in a single gulp and sets the glass back down on the table. Noticing the name card beside the glass, he picks it up.

'Jiang . . . hey, that's the same name as yours . . . Mr Jiang Qinglin. Who's Jiang Qinglin?'

For a moment, I panic. What should I say?

'Oh, that . . . well, I don't know him. He . . . he says he's my father.'

'What?' Red looks as if his eyes might pop out of his head.

'Well, he came knocking on the door this morning, looking for me. He says I'm his daughter.'

'But I thought you said you didn't have a father.'

'That's what I thought, too.'

'Where on earth did he come from?'

'I have no idea.'

'But, if you've never met your father, how can you be sure this man really is him?'

Almost unconsciously, I begin moving around, just to have something to do. My mind is a blank as I tidy up, tossing Red's sweaty T-shirt into the washing machine and adding some powder.

But Red wants to know more.

'What did he look like?'

'A bit like me, I suppose.'

'So you look like him, you mean.'

'Especially the hands.'

'Hands? How can you tell if a man is your father just from his hands?'

'And he also called me by my first name. The way he said my name was different, somehow, from the way other people say it.'

'But the way I say your name is different too, isn't it?'

Red seems unwilling to accept such a sudden turn of events.

'He came to tell me that he has cancer. The doctors say that he only has two months to live.'

'Oh?' Red seems rather sceptical. 'He's probably just some old con artist looking for a handout.'

'Could be.'

'Or maybe he's really sick, and is just looking for someone to take care of him in the hospital.'

'Possibly, but he said he doesn't expect me to take care of him. He just wanted to see me once, that's all.'

Puzzled, Red ceases his questioning and goes into the kitchen for a lemon soda. After taking a few sips, he resumes his contemplation of the man who claims to be my father.

'Let me get this straight, Coral. A strange man with hands a bit like yours comes to our door this morning looking for you, and tells you he's the father you've never met before. You see from his card that he has the same surname as you. Then he tells you that he has terminal cancer and has only two months left to live, but he says he doesn't expect you to take care of him. And then he just leaves, without asking you for anything.'

I nod, unsure where Red is going with this analysis or what conclusion he is heading towards.

But he is making no conclusions.

'And just like that, he left,' Red mumbles to himself.

'Yes, he just left,' I answer disappointedly. This seems to be the only point we can agree upon.

'You should consider him gone, then. Just pretend he was never here.'

I do not answer. The man may have been a stranger, but he came to see me. He wouldn't have come to see me if he hadn't needed me. If I am going to ignore the unexpected visit, I might as well pretend that it was a dream. A dream that I have woken from, a dream that I related to Red when he came home from playing Frisbee.

If I can't forget about the brief encounter, I think to myself, I will just pretend that it was a dream.

20

Flipping through the calendar, I notice that the date is 14 August, or the fifteenth day of the seventh moon of the lunar calendar. We are currently reaching the end of the thirteenth solar term, called Autumn's Beginning, and in a few days will enter the fourteenth, the Limit of Heat. The city is moving into autumn. The dew on the grass, the colour of the leaves, the rhythm of the breeze, the height of the sun in the sky, the shape of the moon – all are testaments to a season's quiet passage. It is the time of year when a hush seems to fall over the city and the weather, usually so harsh and arid, takes on a kinder, gentler mood. Autumn is the only season that Red and I, as residents of this city, really enjoy. But this autumn feels different. I look at the red circles I have drawn on the calendar to mark my period days. My last period was a month and a half ago. My breasts are swollen and painful. I feel frightened. I don't know exactly what I am frightened of, only that it is not an external type of fear. It is coming from inside me, a profound loneliness that has seeped into the very marrow of my bones.

Thinking about my little home town one thousand eight hundred kilometres away, I realise that in the Village of Stone, the seventh moon was always a season of destruction. For the villagers, the seventh moon was neither summer nor autumn. It was the season of hurricanes, the season of death. But it was also the season when the catch was at its best. Crabs, for instance, had to be caught before the autumn set in. Once the autumn winds began to blow, the crabs lost their freshness and their flesh grew slack.

I look at the calendar again and read through the explanatory notes at the bottom of the page:

Inauspicious Omens:
Drinking spirits, planting crops,
opening storehouses, entering into contracts.

Auspicious Omens:
Memorial services, funereal offerings,
cleaning ovens and chimneys, changing seasonal clothes.

I request some time off work so that Red and I can go to the hospital together.

Red takes a seat beside three other men on a green bench outside the obstetrics and gynaecology department. With their furrowed brows and haggard faces, they look like a line-up of the world's four most wretched men. The bench looks ancient, much of its green paint already chipped away. I wonder how many men have sat on the bench over the years, waiting for their women to emerge from the doorway marked 'OB/GYN'.

In the hospital toilet, I urinate into a small plastic cup and take the urine sample to the lab. Ten minutes later, I receive my test results, a slip of paper with a red stamp that reads: 'Pregnancy test: Positive'.

I go back into the waiting room, walk over to the green bench and hand the slip of paper to Red.

He glances at it, but says nothing.

'They said that if we're in a hurry, we can get rid of it today,' I tell him. 'I'll go in and talk to the doctor now, and they should be able to fit me in right away.'

Red remains silent. What is he thinking? Or is he thinking anything at all?

I take the slip of paper from his hand and begin to walk away.

'What are you doing?' Red sounds agitated.

I answer him calmly. 'I'm going to talk to the doctor.'

'About what?'

'About the operation and when they can do it.'

With this, I walk into the doctor's examination room.

The doctor is a compassionate-looking woman who seems as if she is quite used to dealing with women who have got themselves into trouble.

'There are two different methods available,' she tells me very matter-of-factly. 'One is a drug-induced abortion, the other is surgical.'

'Which one hurts less?' I enquire, shamefacedly.

'If you have a reasonable tolerance for discomfort, neither is particularly painful.' The doctor looks up from my case history and fixes me with a frank gaze. 'I see here that you've had an abortion before, so you should know what to expect. Of course, that was a decade ago, when it wasn't common practice to use anaesthesia, but the surgical procedure is more or less the same today.'

I nod my head.

'A drug-induced abortion happens in two stages, and is suitable for pregnancies that have not progressed beyond the sixth week, assuming the patient has no serious medical conditions or other complications. First we administer one thousand five hundred milligrams of mifepristone, then forty-eight hours later, six hundred milligrams of misoprostol. This will shrink the foetus, and cause some abdominal pain and vaginal bleeding, but most patients expel the foetus within six hours. At this stage, the foetus is nothing more than a small whitish lump. We'll give you a small glass bottle so that you can bring it in afterwards for examination. It can take up to a week for some women to expel the foetus, although this happens in only a small number of cases. Some patients experience side effects from the drugs used in the procedure. The most common side effects are nausea, diarrhoea and mild fever. After a drug-induced abortion, there is usually a fair amount of bleeding, which can continue for ten to fifteen days afterwards. Drug-induced abortions have a slightly lower success rate than surgical abortions, but the difference is negligible.'

After a slight pause, the doctor continues.

'Surgical abortion is a quicker procedure. These days, the vacuum method is the procedure of choice. Years ago, dilation and curettage was the most common method for terminating early-stage pregnancies, but this has been largely replaced by suction methods. For later-stage pregnancies, the saline solution method is quite effective and still relatively common. This involves a saline solution injected either into the womb or directly into the amniotic sac. Surgical extraction is a method suitable for pregnancies between the tenth and fourteenth week, in cases where other methods are inappropriate. The risks are relatively small, under the following conditions. One: patients should be free of vaginal conditions such as pelvic inflammatory disease, trichomoniasis, yeast or other bacterial infections. Two: patients should be in good physical health, with no history of anaemia, hepatitis, angina, heart failure, problems with kidney function or kidney failure. Three: the procedure cannot be performed on patients with a fever, because if body temperature exceeds thirty-seven and a half degrees, there can be complications. Four: patients should abstain from sexual intercourse for at least three days before the procedure.'

I ponder this in silence while the doctor waits for my reply.

'Which one is cheaper?' I ask haltingly.

'Will your employer be paying your medical expenses?'

'No.'

'In that case, if you're paying for it yourself, the drug-induced method is several hundred yuan cheaper. A surgical abortion costs about sixteen hundred yuan.'

'Then I suppose the drug-induced method is better for me,' I say quietly.

'But I should tell you,' the doctor continues, 'that the drug-induced method is only effective ninety to ninety-five per cent of the time. In a small percentage of cases, the foetus is not expelled completely.' Her tone grows serious. 'In such cases, a surgical abortion is necessary to remove the rest of the foetus. It can be a painful procedure.'

I feel as if my heart has plunged to my stomach.

Red and I walk home from the hospital in silence. I decide to stay home from work for the rest of the day. All that afternoon, I am overcome by a feeling of hopelessness.

Red remains silent.

The cat upstairs meows all through the night, though the rest of the building is deep in sleep. In the silence, broken only by the cat's wailing, the world seems so deserted, so cold and empty. There is nothing left to cling to in this world, nothing I can hold on to.

When I wake, I find myself alone in the bed. I prop myself up on one elbow and look around the bedroom. Red, dressed only in his underwear, is sitting in the wicker chair by the window, smoking in silence.

The smoke, curling softly upwards, is thrown into relief by the early morning sunlight.

Despite our troubles, the sunlight still consents to shine down upon us. That must count for something.

'You're awake,' Red says huskily, as he exhales a plume of smoke. He looks as if he hasn't slept.

'How long have you been up?'

'Quite a while. I got up before dawn.'

'Why so early? Was it the noise from upstairs?' I listen, but the cat seems to have fallen silent. I notice that the entire building is, for once, completely silent.

I can guess what Red is thinking. He must be thinking about going to the hospital together, but is reluctant to bring up the subject.

I sit up and look at my watch. If Red isn't going to say it, I will. I am on the verge of asking him to accompany me to the hospital when he speaks:

'Coral, let's get married.'

Suddenly, the room is a blur of smoke and sunlight. I gaze at Red in confusion, unsure whether I have heard him correctly.

'Let's get married.' He stubs out his cigarette in the ashtray. 'I want us to have this baby, Coral.'

Red stands up from his chair, walks over and takes me in his arms. We hold each other for a long time. Now that we have something to cling to, neither of us wants to let go.

What goes up must comes down. Even a Frisbee has to come back down to earth some time.

21

We don't go back to the hospital.

Red says that when the time comes, we will ask the same kindly doctor to help with the delivery.

We decide not to do an ultrasound, because we do not want to know the sex of the baby in advance. Some things are best left to the sea goddess Mazu Niangniang. Let the goddess decide.

My mood gradually improves. I have something growing inside me that makes me feel warm and full, something that is a part of me, something that links Red and me together as never before.

From the moment Red walks into the employment office and fills in a job application form listing his age as thirty, he stops complaining that jobs are idiotic. While he makes the rounds of job interviews at different companies, his Frisbee rests quietly on top of the wardrobe, as if observing the newfound maturity of its owner.

The salted eel that came all the way from the post office in the Village of Stone spends its days shuttling back and forth between our refrigerator and the chopping board. It feeds us for a long time, through meals of eel on rice, eel in soup, steamed and stir-fried eel and eel braised in soy sauce. Little by little, we whittle down its bulk. Red even goes out and buys a cookbook of eel recipes and then proceeds, through trial and error, to master every one. I begin to believe that we have no cause for worry: even if Red is unable to find work, we would have no trouble finding jobs as chefs in one of Beijing's many upmarket seafood restaurants, because we have more authentic and delicious eel recipes in our repertoire than most professional chefs. For Red, the fishy smell that once proved so unbearable has become the scent of money, a thing of tangible value.

Our lives begin to improve. In the process of digesting our daily meals of eel, we regain our spirit and our strength. Thanks to our new, healthier diet, we suffer no more sleepless nights. The eel recipes are having an effect.

The only thing for which there is no consolation is the memory of the elderly man who claimed to be my father. He has not returned, but I think of him often, a nondescript old man living all alone somewhere, suffering from the same ailments that afflict other men his age. Maybe he has liver spots on his neck or a bad back, perhaps he suffers from poor digestion or frequent constipation, maybe he has been forced to give up smoking and is finding it to be a difficult battle. I must have turned his image over in my mind a thousand times, but I cannot find a single negative or hateful thing about him. Everything about him seemed so kind and gentle, particularly his hands, those hands that so resembled mine.

I still have his card. To avoid losing it, I have tucked it into my pocket diary. Yet I hesitate to take it out and look at it again because I know exactly what I will find there. Besides his name and an address that has been blacked out rather ineffectively in felt tip pen, the only other thing on the card is a telephone number.

I still cannot bring myself to decide whether or not to dial that telephone number.

In idle moments, Red and I sometimes talk about the old man. I suggest that perhaps he was telling the truth, that he does only have two months to live. Maybe he is lying alone in a sickbed in a hospital somewhere, with only an IV drip and an oxygen tube to keep him company. When I start talking like this, Red always tries to change the subject. He points out that because I have always considered my father dead, his sudden visit was more like the visitation of a ghost or spirit than a real person. My father was nothing more than a ghost who came to seek my forgiveness.

I resolve not to think any further about the elderly man who stood, alive and in the flesh, in my front hall that morning. There are plenty of other things to think about. During the day, my melancholy thoughts are effectively drowned out by the noise of our building, these twenty-five storeys filled with other people, other lives.

But when I am alone, when Red has gone out to buy a newspaper or some milk, and silence settles over the apartment block, I once again find myself plunged into reflection. Try as I might, I cannot convince myself to forget the old man who came to my house claiming to be my father. His words ring in my head:

'Coral, I have cancer. They say it's terminal.'

I try to rationalise by telling myself that this man, Jiang Qinglin, is simply one of countless old men out there dying of cancer. But these comforting excuses disappear the minute I feel the life growing in my belly. At these times, I feel a sense of responsibility, the responsibility that one human being feels for another.

I can talk myself out of it no longer. I dig out the card the old man has left, and dial his telephone number.

My hand trembles as I hold the telephone receiver. I am already regretting my impulsive decision, made in a moment of haste. I am happy with my life the way it is, and I am aware that I could be plunging myself into a great deal of trouble by making this call.

While I mull this over in my mind, the phone on the other end of the line continues to ring. The ringing seems to go on for ages. After what seems like an eternity, someone answers.

'Hello,' I say, 'I'm looking for Jiang Qinglin.'

A crude and unfamiliar male voice replies, 'Who?'

'Jiang Qinglin.'

'There's nobody called that here!' the man says rudely.

'Isn't your address 30 Jintai Road?'

'Yeah.' The man on the other end of the line sounds impatient.

'Well, this is the number someone gave me on a business card.'

'We're a guest house.'

'A guest house? Oh, I see. Have you had a man named Jiang Qinglin, thin, about sixty years old, check in recently?'

'What business is it of yours?' the man on the other end asks suspiciously.

'I . . . I'm his daughter and I'm trying to find him.' What else can I say? It is the only thing that comes to mind.

'I think he might have been here about a week ago, but he isn't staying here now. He's already left.'

'Do you know where he went?'

The man slams the phone down. He must not have replaced the phone in the cradle properly, though, because when I press the receiver to my ear I can hear the slap of the man's slippers echoing down what sounds like a long empty hallway. Judging from the acoustics, the place must be deserted, or perhaps it is simply one of those inexpensive guest houses installed in a basement somewhere. Finally, the footsteps fade and all I can hear is the faint buzzing of the telephone line. There is something surreal about it, as if I have reached a number that exists in no real time or space.

I hang up and study the card again. Other than the telephone number and a vaguely legible address, it contains no useful information.

I think about Jiang Qinglin all day, and at night I dream that he is standing by my bed. He has been transformed into an angel with a pair of snow-white wings sprouting from his back. Though he says nothing, only stands and stares at me, I can see in his eyes that he needs my forgiveness. I nod to him, wordlessly, and it seems as if a great weight has been lifted from his shoulders. Yes, I can forgive him. But what other sins has this man – this man who claims to be my father – committed in his lifetime? As soon as I have forgiven him, he flies through the window, his body carried away on wings of white.

When I wake to the faint light of dawn, I feel frightened by a dark premonition. I look at Red lying next to me, deep in sleep. Unable to wait for him to wake up on his own, I shake him until he opens his eyes. He does not seem particularly happy to have been woken so early.

'I have to go and see Jiang Qinglin,' I tell him.

Red stares at me in confusion, but at least this time he does not try to talk me out of it.

I take the card from my diary again and glance at the address. This time, I decide, I will go directly to the guest house.

The guest house is in a basement, just as I guessed. It is deserted, save for a few traders with business in Beijing who appear to live in the guest house all year round. By the look of them, they are mainly poor pedlars, the sort of failed middle-aged men who make a modest living buying and selling whatever wares they can find. Through open doors, I can hear water being poured from a thermos, a man yawning, all the sounds of loneliness and failure. The rooms are spartanly furnished, containing only a bed, a pair of plastic slippers, a table, a hot water thermos and glass, a washbasin and a fluorescent lamp. Besides the communal sinks and bathrooms, further down the corridor, there are no other amenities. Although the guest house is underground, there is still some faint sunlight visible through the windows. It is more of a half-basement really, with windows at street level from which you can see people's feet as they walk past. The air is permeated with the odour of damp and mould. Perhaps because they are left on twenty-four hours a day, the lights in the corridor are very low wattage, more suited to feline vision than to human eyes. When someone passes down the corridor, their footsteps echo from end to end, and the dim lights overhead cast vague shadows along the walls. The man at the reception desk, perhaps the same man who answered my phone call, ignores me, keeping his eyes glued to a television programme he is watching on a set with exceedingly poor reception. I finally manage to glean some information from one of the other boarders, who says he works in the pharmaceutical trade. He tells me that Jiang Qinglin has left the guest house and moved into a hospital for terminal cancer patients.

I know that there are two cancer hospitals in Beijing, so I follow my intuition and go to the one I know specialises in late-stage cancer treatment. The hospital deals with cases in which the cancer has spread so badly that there is not much hope for a cure. It is not so much a cancer treatment centre as a hospice, intended to make the patients as comfortable as possible while they wait for death. Just as I suspected, Jiang Qinglin is a patient there.

There is no mistake. His name is right there in the hospital registration book: Jiang, Qinglin.

I enter my own name in the visitors' book: Jiang, Coral.

Jiang and Jiang. Between these two names, I wonder, does there really exist some connection, some inescapable and unavoidable link?

When I finally get to see Jiang Qinglin, he is about to be operated on. He is lying on a hospital trolley and is dressed in a sterile paper gown. Even his feet have been wrapped in sterile blue paper bags. Because he has been sedated, he is unable to talk or move. As I enter, the nurses are just wheeling him into the operating theatre.

I do not even have the chance to talk to the old man. He cannot see or hear me.

I tell the nurses that I am his daughter and ask them to let me into the theatre, but they inform me that no one is allowed in during the operation.

The door closes behind them, the red light over it goes on and I am left to wait outside. It is a long wait. I feel nervous somehow, as if the last judgement were already at hand, but I know that there is nothing I can do but wait.

When the nurse comes out some time later, I ask her what is happening. She tells me that the operation will take several hours.

I ask her what is wrong with him. She says that he has throat cancer, but it has already spread to the lymphatic system and now his body is filled with tumours. The surgery will excise the most life-threatening parts, but there is nothing that the doctors can do about the other tumours, short of chemotherapy. The prognosis is grim.

I sit outside the main door to the surgical department, watching patients being wheeled back and forth.

When the nurse emerges from the theatre a second time, she seems rather curious about me. 'Are you really his daughter?' she asks.

What am I supposed to say?

I nod my head.

'That's very odd,' the nurse replies, taken aback. 'If you are his daughter, how can you not have known he has cancer?'

I struggle to find a plausible answer. 'Well, you see . . . we've only met once.'

The nurse seems even more surprised. 'Well, well . . . that's one I haven't heard before. Before sending a patient in for serious surgery, this hospital usually requires a signature by a family member or close friend. But in his case, he had no one to sign for him. We just assumed he had no living relatives.'

'What did you do?'

'In the end, the head doctor gave his approval because it is such an urgent case. Without surgery, he wouldn't make it through another week.'

With this, the nurse hurries back to her duties.

Seven hours later, the operation is finished and the anaesthetic is beginning to wear off. The old man has regained partial consciousness. He has been wheeled out of the theatre and into the intensive care ward, which already houses several other patients.

The nurse warns me that when the anaesthetic wears off completely, the old man will be in a great deal of pain.

I stand at his bedside staring at his face. His wrinkled neck and haggard face make him look so very old. Even in his semi-conscious state, he is grimacing, his brows knit with pain. I can see the hole in his throat where they have cut out the tumour. The hole seems to extend all the way through, as if his throat has been hollowed out completely. I can almost see the blood moving slowly through his blood vessels and filling the dark hole, as if emptying into an open grave. When at last he regains full consciousness, he opens his eyes and looks at me. Our eyes meet. I think he must recognise me, for the minute he sees me, his eyes fill with tears.

At that moment, a nurse carrying a bottle of medicine enters the room.

The old man opens his mouth as if to say something, but no sound comes out. At the very same moment, he and I realise that he can't speak.

The nurse hastens to explain. 'They had to remove his vocal cords.'

Stunned, I glance back at the old man and see the hopelessness in his eyes. He looks just like a frightened child.

He raises his hand and weakly signals for something to write on. I pull some paper out of my backpack and the nurse hands him a pen. He places the paper on the sheet over his chest and begins to write something. Though he is unable to see the paper and his hand is trembling, he manages to scrawl the following words: 'It hurts.'

I feel a lump in my throat, and know that I can contain myself no longer. I pick up the paper and rush from the hospital ward. Before I am out of the door, I am choked with sobs. Outside in the corridor filled with doctors walking back and forth on their errands, I stand and weep.

When I realise that my sobs are audible, I press my hand against my mouth. The last thing I want is for the old man in his hospital bed to hear me outside crying.

When night falls, I keep a vigil at his bedside. Because he cannot speak, and is so weak with pain that he isn't even able to write, no words pass between us. Just after 2 a.m., the family members gathered around the next bed begin crying. The patient has died. Two nurses quickly wheel his body from the room.

After that, the bed next to us is empty. The old man stays awake most of the night, as do I. Perhaps he is too frightened to sleep. In the silence of the emergency ward, we have our thoughts to ourselves. Fear of death and the primal desire for survival are never far from our minds. I give the old man my hand, for I know that he needs me. After all, what else in this world can he cling to?

He grips my hand tightly, as if he is trying to hold on to an entire world. We sit like this for a long time, neither of us saying a word. He has lost his voice and I am afraid to speak. I know that if I open my mouth, I will start crying right in front of him.

In the morning, a nurse comes into the ward and inserts a long plastic feeding tube into the old man's nose. It must be painful, for he keeps opening and closing his mouth and seems to be having trouble breathing. Using a large syringe, the nurse feeds a mixture of egg and corn soup into the tube and down into his stomach.

At about noon, the old man finally has the urge to urinate. Because he is still weak and partially paralysed from the surgery, he is unable to do so. The pain must be excruciating, for his entire body is soaked with sweat, his face flushed a deep red and his breathing erratic. The doctor said that it was important for the patient to urinate after surgery, in order to expel the toxins from his system. A build-up of toxins can cause serious complications. The two nurses try everything they can think of to help. They pour water into glasses in the hope that the sound will encourage him to urinate, but even the faint sound of running water proves unbearable and excruciatingly painful for the old man. Two hours later, the doctor decides that the only option is to use a catheter. The process is unpleasant to watch, and involves another long plastic tube.

Early in the evening, the old man wakes and the nurse comes

in to give him his liquid food. She teaches me how to use the syringe and feeding tube, so that I can help feed him when the nurses are not around. Following the nurse's example, I practise clearing the air from the tube and testing the temperature and consistency of the liquid to make sure it is neither too hot nor too cold, too thin nor too thick. Then I try my first feed.

I have not yet mastered the technique. A few times I feed the liquid through the tube too quickly, causing the old man to choke. His silent choking terrifies me. Though he makes no sound, his face grows very red, his upper body begins to tremble and I can see the fear in his eyes.

Later that night, we repeat the same process – another catheter, more food, and finally, the dawn of a new day . . .

The third evening is deathly silent, and the old man remains in a semi-comatose state. The silence so frightens me that I resolve to go out the next day and buy a radio, just to relieve the silence and give him something to listen to while lying in bed. But as the old man's condition grows more critical, I know that I will never have the chance. He dies at 6.20 a.m., just before dawn.

The nurses immediately remove the feeding tube from his nose and disconnect the IV drip. They wheel away his hospital bed, and I release his hand for the last time.

There are so many things that I did not have time to tell him. He will never know that my grandfather named me Little Dog because it was a lucky nickname, a talisman that would prevent the Sea Demon from snatching me from the shore.

It is too late to tell him anything now. I had hoped, when his condition stabilised, to tell him about my grandparents, about all the things that happened in our three-storey house of stone, and about why their Little Dog had to leave the village. Even if he wasn't really my father, even if he knew nothing about the Village of Stone, he came to find me before he died, and I sat by his bedside and held his hand. He seemed to know and understand me. His death brought us together, caused our fates to intertwine. And I am pregnant.

But it is too late to tell him that, too.

I sign my name to the old man's death certificate. Time of death: 6.20 a.m. Witness: Coral Jiang.

As I emerge from the hospital, I glance upwards and see that the sky is tinged with a faint red. It is late afternoon already and the intersections are thronged with bicyclists, pedalling with supreme indifference through traffic signals. I am still enveloped in the antiseptic smell of the hospital. I shed no tears. No longer do I feel plagued by unresolved questions about my father and my childhood in the Village of Stone. When I was growing up, I so hated that village and everything about it: the coldness of its inhabitants, the endless typhoons, the crumbling houses on the mountainside, my grandfather's cruelty to my grandmother and, most of all, the secret shame of my experiences with the mute. But now I feel my hatred ebbing away. I realise that there is something cold about my hatred of the village, something as cold and cruel as the deaths that befell the village each year during the seventh moon. It is a hatred without reason. After all, what logical reason can a person have for hating a *place*?

In truth, I *did* love some of the people in my home town. And as I watched that old man dying in the hospital, I realised that I retain some nostalgia for the Village of Stone, despite its constant typhoons and fishing boats dashed to pieces against the rocks. Because I held that old man's hand and waited with him for death, I find that I can hate no longer. It is as if my love has finally been repaid. At last, the accounts are even.

22

A week after my father – or perhaps I should say the man who might have been my father – passed away, Red and I finish our last piece of salted eel. We have averaged about two portions per day, not a bad pace for such an enormous and overpoweringly salty piece of seafood. Red even took to making eel sandwiches garnished with crispy slices of lettuce. It sounds a strange sort of sandwich, but it was actually quite a delicious combination. Sometimes I packed rice and bits of steamed eel into a plastic lunchbox to take to work with me so that I could eat my lunch in the video shop while I advised customers on the latest movies and new releases. I doubt that the manager was particularly happy about having a video shop that smelled of eel, but I enjoyed my lunches. In this way, the eel fed us through the summer.

Now that the eel is gone, the cat upstairs has stopped meowing.

Red and I feel as if something important has disappeared from our lives. We sniff around the kitchen, hoping to find some trace of the old familiar smell on the chopping boards, pots and pans, white porcelain bowls and plastic lunchboxes. We hold them up to our noses, hoping that some last vestige of the scent might remain. But the pungent smell of eel, an odour so like the sea of the Village of Stone, a scent that Red said reminded him of a woman's vagina, is fading from our rooms with each passing day. It leaves in its wake an emptiness that seems to permeate everything. Something has changed in our lives, and now our lives need another change, something new to fill the void.

Red and I have muddled through the summer's blistering heat like two wild animals slumbering in their mountain caves. Now that we have awoken, our first impulse is to escape our towering block of flats, this gigantic prison cell, and go out for a walk.

We have no idea where we are going, nor do we care. All we want is to get out of our high-rise. We wander, directionless, down to the street. The sky above is clear and blue. The silver spokes spinning beneath bicyclists' feet glint metallic in the autumn sunlight. The green leaves of the poplar trees cast dappled shadows on the ground below. And then there are the 'scholar' trees, so silent and fragile, shedding their pale yellow blossoms, carpeting the pavement, and even the passersby, with flower petals. Idlers sitting at the kerbside reading newspapers soon find their shoulders cloaked with yellow petals.

We spend hours wandering around the city and go to Liulichang, our favourite antiques street, to look at jade ornaments and other curios. We buy freshly roasted sweet potatoes from a man who cooks them over a large metal drum. The sweet potatoes are so piping hot that we have to blow on the orange flesh to cool it. I stop to admire the miniature carvings and delicate cut-paper pictures being sold on the street. The stone carvings are about the size of a thumb and wrapped in festive red paper. I examine the tiny scenes with a magnifying glass; there are classical Chinese landscapes and scholars in their long Chinese robes. Red waits beside me, munching on his sweet potato and gazing back down the length of the narrow street filled with antiques. The mournful coo of pigeons fills the air and echoes from the glazed tile rooftops.

Red stands beneath one of the ancient scholar trees that still line this street and cocks his head as if he is listening to something. Then he turns to me and says, 'The blossoms are falling. I can hear them.'

'What?'

'The blossoms. I can hear them falling.'

Red pops the last bit of sweet potato into his mouth and keeps walking.

Two weeks later, Red finds a job writing a regular column for a sports magazine. It is the perfect job for him, and he has already written several Frisbee-related pieces for the same magazine. On the subject of Frisbee, Red is an expert without equal.

Now that Red has a job and we can finally afford a new flat, we consider moving. But every time the subject comes up, I begin to feel a bit reluctant to leave. I have lived in the flat for a long time and it holds so many memories. If we move, I will miss all the things that once annoyed me. I would even miss the small corner of the balcony, with its brief forty-five minute spells of sunlight.

After many days of indecision, Red finally puts an end to the discussion. 'I don't want us to live like hermit crabs any more,' he says. 'We should buy a little house of our own.'

I agree, mostly because I like the way he says it.

Just before the end of autumn, Red and I borrow all the money we can to buy a small house in the hills west of Beijing where property is very cheap. We are thrilled to have found a place in the countryside, where we will have more early morning sunshine and fresh air. When the weather is pleasant, we can climb to the top of the hill and gaze at the Great Wall snaking off into the distance.

I decide to try my hand at sports, rather than simply standing on the sidelines and watching. I start playing Frisbee, and have soon begun to grasp the intricacies of Red's tournament rules. For example, there are seven players to each team, and it is important for the players to work together to keep possession of the Frisbee. The team that manages to keep the Frisbee from touching the ground and acquire the most points by throwing it into the end zone is the winner. If the Frisbee touches the ground or is intercepted by the other team, possession changes to the opposing team. The main things to remember are not to move your feet when you have possession of the Frisbee and, most importantly, to hang on to it for dear life.

Meanwhile, tremendous changes are taking place within my body. I am emerging from my cave. I begin to realise that my body is still young, and that I am capable of handing down warmth and love to another human being. My baby will not be a second-generation hermit crab. He or she will inherit a new start.

As winter approaches, the forested hills around our house turn a brilliant red. The late autumn frosts set in, turning the leaves an even deeper shade of vermilion. A single gusty night can blow away half of the leaves. Far from all of the sounds of the city, Red and I sit outside our doorway and look out at the hills covered in green bristlegrass. I turn to Red and tell him that I want to go back.

'Go back?' he asks. 'Go back where?'

'To the Village of Stone. I want to go back and see it again.'

'Are you sure?' Red sounds dubious.

'I'm sure.'

'This is the same Village of Stone that the eel came from?' I nod.

'All right,' he says, 'but I'm going with you. And I'll bring my Frisbee, too.'

We burst out laughing at the same time.

23

We leave Beijing and travel three days and nights by train. The days and nights seem endless, the mountain tunnels interminable, but at long last, we emerge from beneath the mountain and I see my childhood village.

We disembark at the long-distance bus station. The station is in the same location I remember, but no longer is it the tiny kingdom over which the old stationmaster reigned supreme. The staff of one has expanded to include ticket takers, ticket sellers and timetablers. The three vomit-splattered buses have been displaced by a whole fleet of new buses, of different makes and models. The old stationmaster is nowhere to be seen, but I do catch a glimpse of a young man dressed in a white T-shirt and tight blue jeans who is his spitting image. The man stands in one corner of the depot, giving instructions to the staff. I notice that the bus timetable in the waiting room now lists frequent departures to and from most of the major cities in China, and that the bus station yard is filled with long-distance coaches from all over. These days, traversing the mountains is a simple matter for the village fishermen. They can go anywhere they want and come back again whenever they wish.

Red and I stay in the Village of Stone for three days.

There is nothing hidden, nothing artful in the sea or in the snaking, narrow alleyways laid out so guilelessly before Red's eyes. I wonder what secrets of my past incarnation those cobblestone streets might be trying to communicate to him. I watch Red's face carefully for any change of expression, but he seems as placid and silent as ever. He doesn't ask me a single question.

It is as if Red has been here before, as if he somehow already knows this place.

Number 13 Pirate's Alley. My childhood house is still standing, the same as always. It is the same three-storey house of stone that I remember, with the same termite-riddled wooden front door and cramped, narrow staircase, the same small second-floor window looking out at the ocean. Even the charred electricity pole listing outside the front door is the same. I can still see my grandmother, dressed in mourning black, clinging to the pole and weeping for her dead husband, and the crowd of fishermen's wives clustered around the coffin, gossiping about us.

The old wooden dining table still occupies the same place in the downstairs kitchen, although the familiar pot of shrimp paste has disappeared.

It is the scene of my childhood, but it is no longer my childhood home. My grandfather's chamber pot and creaky bamboo bed are gone, as are my grandmother's vat of water and her statues of Guanyin and Mazu. The village housing authority says that the house still belongs to me, although in the interim, they have lent it to a young couple who run a hairdresser's shop. When I visit the house, the couple are not at home, so I don't get the chance to meet them. But I do meet their son, a seven- or eight-year-old boy who is downstairs watching television. I notice that the television stands in exactly the same place my grandmother used to keep her statues. The rough stone walls have been covered with a new coat of white paint, and now boast a large poster advertising imported French hair dye. The wall formerly occupied by the sideboard is taken up by a large plastic hairdryer and two large mirrors mounted side by side. Below the mirrors, there is a counter cluttered with scissors and combs of various shapes and sizes.

The boy tells me that his parents have gone to market. I cannot remember what day of the lunar calendar it is, so I am unsure whether it is a regular village market day, or some special event or village fair. My sense of time is geared to the modern calendar of city life, rather than to the lunar calendar of the villagers.

Next door, Boy Waiting's family still has the same small court-yard and flowering jasmine tree, but their seven daughters have grown up and moved away. After Boy at Last died, Boy Waiting's parents never succeeded in having a son. The six older sisters have husbands and children of their own now, and Boy Waiting has married a young man from a neighbouring village. He is not a fisherman, but an employee at the local seafood cold processing plant. Their life together seems happy and tranquil. Boy Waiting's older sister, Golden Phoenix, spent several years performing with the provincial theatre troupe until she grew too old to continue playing the ingénue roles and returned to the village, where they had established a new opera troupe. Golden Phoenix was put in charge of their scenery and theatrical props. She married an actor known for his lead role in the opera *Tiger King: Thief of Hearts*, thus fulfilling her parents' prophecy that she would fall in love with an actor. After retiring from the stage, her husband was promoted to director of the village theatre troupe, and is now considered a bit of a local celebrity. Boy Waiting's father, the Captain, has finally retired after a lifetime spent at sea. Though he has recently celebrated his seventy-third birthday and seems quite elderly, he cannot quite bear to sell his fishing boat. He puts a new coat of paint on the boat every year and rents it out to some young men in the village in return for a percentage of their annual profits. As long as he still has his boat, he will always be the Captain.

Although the Captain is no longer a fisherman, he enjoys repeating his favourite maritime saying:

'The only thing separating a sea scavenger from the Sea Demon is three inches of wooden plank.'

Boy Waiting's mother is still alive and well. I don't know whether she still grieves over the loss of her youngest child, her Boy at Last.

Nobody brings up the topic of Mr Mou while I am there, but I am sure that he leads the same normal life as the other men in the village. He must have a house and children. Perhaps he is still teaching at the village school, or maybe he has found a different job by now. In my heart he is still beautiful and pure, quiet and peaceful, the same Mr Mou who stood with me on that moonlit mountaintop. I have no wish to disturb him or to talk about him or even to see him again. He occupies a special place in my heart, a quiet corner where he can live on, forever undisturbed.

One new addition to the village is a high breakwater constructed on the seashore. I hear that it does little to protect the village from typhoons, and that the high waves still manage to flow over the breakwater and threaten the stone houses on the other side.

The breakwater extends all the way to the foot of the mountain. On the mountaintop, incense smoke continues to waft from the Temple of the Sea Goddess, although these days her supplicants are few and far between. Her statue seems to have fallen into decrepitude, the face blackened with age, as if it has been many years since the villagers last bothered to add a new coat of gold leaf. I don't know why, but her face looks different somehow, not at all the kind and merciful visage I recall.

Walking along the beach one day, I am puzzled to notice that all the fishing boats seem to be returning home empty-handed, the piles of silvery fish I remember from my childhood conspicuously absent from their decks. When I enquire about the whereabouts of the catch, the fishermen tell me that the boats no longer bring their catch ashore. Instead, they take it directly to the seafood cold processing plant to be frozen and shipped.

Down by the wharf, a large placard hung from the door of the maritime broadcasting station and a loudspeaker mounted on the roof provide the villagers with the most up-to-date weather forecasts and storm warnings. The village fishermen, it seems, are no longer entirely at the mercy of the elements. The wharf is much busier than I remember it. Fleets of fishing boats now ply the coast, their whistles reverberating through my eardrums and echoing down the narrow alleyways of the village.

On the far side of the mountain, I find my grandparents' head-stones, side by side. The graves are overgrown by clumps of wild grasses and the topsoil has eroded, weathered away by the ocean winds. Both plots are so choked with weeds that they appear to have grown together, merged at last into a single grave. I am unsure whether I ought to pull up the weeds or leave them in their natural state. The graves are surrounded by wild straw-berries in bloom, berries so ripe that they have turned almost black, as if they have been ripening here for thousands of years. As I stand beside the graves, I realise that my grandparents always were and always will be inseparable. In life they occupied sep-arate floors, one above the other, but they always shared the same front door. In death they occupy adjacent graves, but they still share the very same patch of earth. Their headstones are surrounded by rows of newly whitewashed grave markers that have expanded to cover the entire hillside.

The mute was buried here as well, in the same cemetery as my grandparents. I have no idea which headstone belongs to him, because I never knew his real name. None of the villagers ever called him anything but 'the mute'. As I stand in that grave-yard, I feel a sudden shiver of fear at the thought of having trodden on his grave without even realising it. I ponder my feelings about the mute and wonder whether he deserves the same things that any dead sinner is entitled to, the same pity and compassion. If I have known misfortune in my life, it is fair to say that he knew even greater misfortune. Now, twenty years later, I still have the power to speak, to write my story, to voice the ocean of hatred I feel towards him. But the mute lost his language and his life. He will lie buried in this cem-etery for all eternity, powerless to speak, as silent in death as he was during his wretched life. If there really is an afterlife, I hope that the mute will be reincarnated as a person with the power

177

of speech, so that he can know how it feels to speak, to scream and to cry.

I feel a profound grief, as if my heart is filled with sorrow. It is a sorrow that emanates from these graves, these graves marked with names I know and names I will never know. I grieve for the dead. I have grown up, moved away from the village and become an adult woman. But none of the occupants of this cemetery will ever know this. I want to offer something to each one of them, some sort of memorial, no matter how frightening or hateful they were while alive. All that is left of their lives is this yellow earth, this ancient soil.

I stand in the cemetery on the far side of the mountain and weep. As the harsh ocean winds buffet my skin, I feel the tears streaming down my face, falling to the parched, dry earth below.

On my last day in the village, I face in the direction of the mountain cemetery, kneel down and touch my head to the ground. There, buried in the shadow of the Temple of the Sea Goddess, on that hillside looking out to sea, are the souls who will live on for ever in my heart.

Coda

I would like to relate one final story, an incident that happened on our last day in the Village of Stone.

It was late afternoon, and Red and I were playing Frisbee on a beach strewn with endless piles of fishing nets. The sea and sky seemed boundless. Wave upon wave rolled up onto the beach, and the seabirds, every bit as carefree as I remembered, flitted back and forth through the foaming whitecaps. Red played happily along the shore, tossing the Frisbee first to me, then out to sea, then wading into the water to retrieve it while I looked on from drier ground. Suddenly I saw the Frisbee spinning through the air, being carried far out to sea by the breeze. It hovered for a moment before plunging into the water, lit gold by the setting sun. Red dived into the ocean and swam out to retrieve his beloved Frisbee, but he could not find it anywhere. He must have searched for the better part of half an hour, but all he could see was crashing waves and sea spray.

I stood upon the rocks at the shore and helped him search, but I could see nothing.

I had a feeling that Red's prized Frisbee would not be coming back.

As for the Frisbee itself, its history and vital statistics are as follows: regulation size, professional class disc especially designed for tournament use. White in colour, with a picture of a green banyan tree on the top, weighing one hundred and forty grams and measuring twenty-six centimetres in diameter. It has been with Red for longer than I have; six years to be exact. It has won forty-three Chinese Frisbee tournaments and two inter-national friendship tournaments. It ended its brilliant career with a burial at sea in the Village of Stone.

If the sea could swallow up Red's prized Frisbee so easily, I wondered, could it also swallow up my Village of Stone?

I began to fear rising sea levels, the melting of the polar ice caps and the expansion of the Arctic Ocean. I was afraid that some day those frigid waters would engulf the Village of Stone and wash away all proof of my memory, all evidence of the place I came from. It makes no difference how far we travel or where we go, but it is important to be perfectly clear about where we come from.

It was almost midnight by the time Red and I struggled out of Beijing's main train station with our luggage, the salt scent of sea air still clinging to our skin and clothing. The sound of the station clock striking midnight echoed up and down Changan Boulevard, the city's main thoroughfare. This was our city, Beijing. Tiananmen Square stretched to the east, the Fragrant Hills to the west. We managed to catch the very last bus, the bus that would bring us back to our home in the suburbs west of the city. From the windows of our bus, speeding through the darkened city, the streetlamps looked like an endless string of tiny fireworks. Looming up ahead, I saw the familiar old twenty-five-storey block of flats. The enormous high-rise that I had once hated so vehemently now seemed welcome and familiar, like a hated friend, or a beloved enemy. As it receded from view and drew back into the depths of the night, its windows still gave off a faint, warm glow. I wondered about the people living in those rooms behind their tiny windows. Behind which windows were there people still awake, people talking, people waiting for lovers not yet returned? I felt as if I knew their secrets, as if I could feel their joys and their sorrows.

I rested my head on Red's shoulder. When the bus shud-dered, I felt the baby move inside my belly, kicking, stretching, reaching out with tiny hands. With the pain came a moment of anxiety, pre-natal jitters or something else. The feeling was bittersweet, both gratifying and sorrowful.

The road home is a long one. As I walk this road, I recall my grandmother's words: 'Everyone has a past life, a future life and a present life.' If that is true, I feel as if my present life has only just begun.

ACKNOWLEDGEMENTS

He lived on the ground floor of a twenty-five-storey building in Beijing. Thanks to Rao Hui for showing me the basement experience, and love.

When I contacted the man who became my agent, Toby Eady, the good woman of China, Xinran, came to test me in Häagen-Dazs, Leicester Square. She had a bunch of flowers with her but not for me. Since then I remind myself again and again that it is still a long journey to carry Chinese fiction to the west. Thanks to both of them for their support, as my agent and friend.

Thanks to Cindy Carter for her lively translation. If she hadn't worked on my book, she would have had more time to perfect her own poetry.

And thanks to Rebecca Carter for her creative editing.